THE UNICORN RESCUE SOCIETY

THE MADRE DE AGUAS OF CUBA

THE UNICORN RESCUE SOCIETY

THE MADRE DE AGUAS OF CUBA

BY **Adam Gidwitz & Emma Otheguy**

ILLUSTRATED BY **Hatem Aly**

CREATED BY **Jesse Casey, Adam Gidwitz, and Chris Lenox Smith**

DUTTON CHILDREN'S BOOKS

DUTTON CHILDREN'S BOOKS

An imprint of Penguin Random House LLC, New York

Text & illustrations copyright © 2020 by Unicorn Rescue Society, LLC.

Penguin supports copyright. Copyright fuels creativity, encourages diverse voices, promotes free speech, and creates a vibrant culture. Thank you for buying an authorized edition of this book and for complying with copyright laws by not reproducing, scanning, or distributing any part of it in any form without permission. You are supporting writers and allowing Penguin to continue to publish books for every reader.

Dutton is a registered trademark of Penguin Random House LLC.

Visit us online at penguinrandomhouse.com

Library of Congress Cataloging-in-Publication Data is available.

Printed in the United States of America
ISBN 9780735231429

1 3 5 7 9 10 8 6 4 2

Edited by Julie Strauss-Gabel
Design by Anna Booth
Text set in ITC Legacy Serif Std

To all my parents.
—A.G.

Para mi familia cubana.
—E.O.

To my cousin Hamada.
—H.A.

UNICORNS ARE REAL.

At least, I think they are.

Dragons are definitely real. I have seen them. Chupa-cabras exist, too. Also Sasquatch. And mermaids—though they are *not* what you think.

But back to unicorns. When I, Professor Mito Fauna, was a young man, I lived in the foothills of Peru. One day, there were rumors in my town of a unicorn in danger, far up in the mountains. At that instant I founded the Unicorn Rescue Society—I was the only member—and set off to save the unicorn. When I finally located it, though, I saw that it was *not* a unicorn, but rather a qarqacha, the legendary two-headed llama of the Andes. I was very slightly disappointed. I rescued it anyway. Of course.

Now, many years later, there are members of the Unicorn Rescue Society all around the world. We are sworn to protect all the creatures of myth and legend. Including unicorns! If we ever find them! Which I'm sure we will!

But our enemies are powerful and ruthless, and we are in desperate need of help. Help from someone brave and kind and curious, and brave. (Yes, I said "brave" twice. It's important.)

Will you help us? Will you risk your very *life* to protect the world's mythical creatures?

Will you join the Unicorn Rescue Society?

I hope so. The creatures need you.

Defende Fabulosa! Protege Mythica!

Mito Fauna, DVM, PhD, EdD, etc.

CHAPTER ONE

Uchenna gazed over the tropical island. Palm trees studded green hillsides. Rivers meandered through valleys. It was the most beautiful island she had ever seen.

Unfortunately, it was only thirteen inches long and nine inches wide, because it had to fit in a baking pan. And it was made out of clay, dirt, twigs, and other materials she and Elliot had found around the playground. But it was *way* nicer than the landscapes of all the other kids in Ms. Vole's class.

Pai Lu, with her black eyeliner and black nail polish and black pants and black shirt and black rings and black combat boots, had made a "blighted waste," as she called it. "Nothing can grow in this cursed land!" she'd announced. "Except for shadows and despair!" Uchenna didn't really get Pai Lu.

Shruti and Janey had made an arctic tundra—which just meant that they had filled their baking pan with ripped-up tissues. Uchenna found this ironic, because Janey constantly had a finger up her nose and Uchenna had *never* seen her use a tissue.

And then there was Jimmy. Jimmy and Jasper and Jhonna had made a big brown lump. Uchenna figured it was supposed to be a mountain, or a hill, or maybe a dung heap. (Which means a pile of poop; Jimmy was *very* into dung heaps.) For some reason, Jimmy was currently sticking pieces of brown clay up one of his nostrils. *Definitely a dung heap,* Uchenna thought.

Just then, Elliot returned to the table with a watering can, grinning. "Ready to see how fresh water systems function on tropical islands?!" he asked.

"I'm kind of more excited to see how Jimmy is going to get that clay out of his nose," Uchenna replied.

"Don't be silly! With these wells, lakes, and underground cave and tunnel systems we've created, we should be able to replicate the true behavior of a water table on a Caribbean island!" Elliot began to sprinkle water over one half of the landscape. Soon, the lakes they'd made began to

fill up. He kept pouring the water—amazingly, the lakes didn't overflow. Instead, water began to appear in tiny wells they'd dug on the *other* side of the island.

"Cool!" Uchenna exclaimed.

"Right?! The water is running through our hidden, subterranean—"

"No," Uchenna interrupted. "Jimmy's trying to shoot the clay out of his nostril by pouring water in the *other* nostril. I guess their project is a geyser?"

Jhonna and Jasper were clapping in rhythm, urging Jimmy on, as he leaned his head back and tried to angle the spout of a water pitcher up his nose. Ms. Vole finally noticed what was happening and hustled over to prevent Jimmy's Nasal Geyser from erupting all over everything.

Just then, the door of the classroom burst open, revealing a tall man with a bushy beard, an enormous shock of black and white hair, and a disheveled tweed suit. His shoulders were rising and falling like he'd been running.

"Excuse me, Ms. Vole!" announced Professor Fauna, in a voice as rich and rocky as the mountains of his native Peru. "I need to borrow—"

Professor Fauna stopped speaking. Ms. Vole had Jimmy bent backwards over her knee, and she was reaching up his nose with her forefinger and thumb.

"Uh, Ms. Vole, what are you doing?"

Ms. Vole looked up like she'd been caught. "Well . . . uh . . . it's a science experiment. . . ."

"Ah. I see. Anywhat, I need to borrow Elliot and Uchenna for the rest of the day."

"For the rest of the day?!" exclaimed Ms. Vole.

"*Urgk!*" said Jimmy, who still had Ms. Vole's fingers up his nose.

"It is *very* important," Professor Fauna assured her. "It's a . . ." He looked at Elliot and Uchenna. They both shrugged. "A science experiment!" he continued. "Like yours! I also have something stuck in my nose-holes! Elliot, Uchenna, follow me!"

As Elliot and Uchenna followed the professor out of the classroom, they heard Janey say, "They get to skip class *again*?"

Shruti replied, "Yeah, but it's always to do weird stuff with that weirdo Professor Fauna. They're going to spend *all day* picking his nose!"

Pai Lu made a gagging face. Janey, whose finger had found its way back up her nose, said, "Yeah, totally gross." Shruti gave her a look. "What?" said Janey. "I don't pick *other* people's noses!"

Jimmy started screaming as Ms. Vole switched to a pipe cleaner to get the clay out of his nasal cavity.

CHAPTER TWO

"¡*Pronto, chibolos!* There is no time to waste!" Professor Fauna led them down the hallway at a brisk pace. Elliot and Uchenna had to hurry to keep up, firing questions as they went.

"Where are we going?" Uchenna had a spring in her step.

Elliot followed her, decidedly less enthusiastic. Professor Fauna was the founder of the Unicorn Rescue Society, a secret organization devoted to keeping the world's mythical creatures safe from danger. Elliot and Uchenna were two of the youngest, and newest, members. They regularly accompanied the professor on his creature-saving missions. Usually, they all almost died. Which was why Elliot was not enthusiastic.

Professor Fauna led the children down two sets of stairs, into the subbasement of the school, and continued striding down a dark hallway, toward a door that used to say JANITORIAL SUPPLIES, but now had a sign taped on it that read, MITO FAUNA, DVM, PHD, EDD, SOCIAL STUDIES DEPARTMENT.

In the few months that they'd been members of the Unicorn Rescue Society, Elliot and Uchenna had already missed a great deal of school in order to travel to distant locations to save dragons and chupacabras and—

"JERSEY!" Elliot yelled. A blue blur bolted out of Professor Fauna's office and slammed into Elliot's chest. Jersey was a blue Jersey Devil with red wings. He was the first mythical creature that Elliot and Uchenna had ever rescued, and he had adopted them. "Come on, little guy, let the sweater live!" Elliot said as he tried to pull Jersey's sharp talons off the cable-knit sweater his grandmother had knit for him. "Bubbe will kill me if this unravels. . . ."

While Elliot wrestled with Jersey in the hallway, Professor Fauna was in his office, gathering up armfuls of old papers from his desk. He even unpinned one from the wall, rolled it up, and shoved it under his armpit. Then, arms overflowing with documents and maps, Professor Fauna pulled the door to his office closed behind him with his shoe.

"Come, come!" he said, *"¡El avión nos espera!"* And, completely blinded by the papers, he made his way down the dark corridor. He walked directly into a large trash can. *"¡Palabrota!"* he muttered and changed course slightly.

"What is going on?" Uchenna asked Elliot, gesturing at Professor Fauna.

Elliot was still trying to get Jersey off his sweater. "What do you mean?" he said. "He's taking us on another reckless mission, in violation of school regulations and probably many national and international child protection laws. . . ." Elliot managed to get Jersey to cling to his face instead of his sweater. "What else is new?"

"No. He's acting even weirder than usual. Professor!" Uchenna called, hurrying after their wiry, wiry-haired mentor. "And what's with all those papers?"

At the end of the hallway, two steps led to a door marked EMERGENCY EXIT ONLY. DO NOT OPEN. ALARM WILL SOUND. Professor Fauna pushed the door open with his hip. No alarm went off. They emerged into the faculty parking lot.

"Looks like it might rain," said Uchenna, stopping and looking at the sky, which was heavy with low-hanging clouds.

"Twenty-five percent chance of a massive storm," Elliot told her. "Up and down the East Coast. It's been all over the weather reports."

"Twenty-five percent chance," said Uchenna. "That's not too bad."

Elliot stared up at the clouds. "Twenty-five percent is a lot! It's the likelihood that a baseball player gets a hit, or that you flip heads in a row two times, or that you step in dog poop in any given year."

Uchenna shot Elliot a look. "You made that last one up."

"I did. But it *feels* right, doesn't it?"

"*¡Vámonos!* Time is of the essence!" Professor Fauna called from the *Phoenix*. His rickety single-propeller plane was parked, as always, between

Ms. Vole's motorcycle and Principal Kowalski's hatchback. The plane was held together by duct tape and, it seemed, good luck. Climbing into the small cabin always made Elliot feel slightly nauseous, whereas taking off and landing always made him feel *violently* nauscous—and scared for his life.

Uchenna pulled open one of the doors. Professor Fauna had flung his load of papers onto the *Phoenix*'s steel floor. Uchenna clambered over them and into her customary seat. Elliot, cursing the day he had joined the Unicorn Rescue Society, climbed in after her, Jersey now clinging to the back of his head. Professor Fauna swung himself in, slammed the door closed behind him, and started the engine. The propeller began to spin.

"*Ahora, mis amigos*, off we go to Miami!"

"Miami?" Uchenna asked. "Is there a magical creature there?"

"No doubt there are many," Professor Fauna answered. "But Miami is just a stop where we will be picking up my dear friend Yoenis. Together, we all shall fly into the Caribbean, to the largest and nearest Caribbean island of them all: Cuba!"

Elliot put his head in his hands. *"Dios mío,"* he sighed.

Professor Fauna turned to him. "Nice use of *español, amiguito.*" He gunned the engine of the *Phoenix* and looked up into the heavy clouds. "Now, I recommend that you fasten your seat belts especially well today."

Elliot groaned.

CHAPTER THREE

As Professor Fauna steered the *Phoenix* toward the end of the school's long driveway, Elliot gripped Uchenna with one hand and his seat belt with the other. "So," he asked, trying to sound nonchalant, "what's happening in Cubaaaaaauuaah!"

Professor Fauna had yanked back on the yoke and the plane was flying up at an extreme and unsafe angle.

"It is complicated," said Professor Fauna.

The back of Elliot's head was buried in the headrest, Jersey was now wrapped around his neck like a scarf, and the plane was still flying straight up into the air. The ominous clouds were now directly ahead of them.

"More complicated than usual?" Uchenna managed to say as the plane finally began to level off. "Rescuing missing dragons and reuniting bloodsucking creatures with their families is pretty complicated. . . ."

"Yes, *claro*," agreed Professor Fauna. "But there are actually *three* reasons we are going to Cuba. First, there is a very bad *sequía* there. A drought. Without enough clean water, people are thirsty, and farms dry up. This is reason number one."

The *Phoenix* entered the clouds and immediately began to jolt and dip—up and down, like a broken carnival ride. Jersey gave Elliot and Uchenna his most pathetic puppy dog expression. His skin was particularly blue.

"He looks airsick," Uchenna said.

The plane jerked up and then dropped down again. Jersey's eyes bulged. He moaned. Then he crawled down to the floor between Elliot's legs.

"Poor little guy," Elliot said, rubbing Jersey's furry blue head.

Uchenna turned back to the professor. "So, what's reason number two?"

"Ah yes! Reason number two for visiting Cuba," Professor Fauna announced, "is that Yoenis's mother, Rosa, has not seen a friend of hers in many weeks."

Uchenna cocked an eyebrow. "Uh . . . is this friend someone special or important?" The Unicorn Rescue Society didn't typically go looking for people's missing friends.

"I would say so," Professor Fauna replied. "Her friend, after all, is a sea serpent."

Uchenna said, "Oh! Cool!"

Elliot moaned, "I have a feeling that this isn't some *nice*, *small*, *SAFE* sea serpent. Am I right?"

Professor Fauna shrugged.

"And what's the third reason we're going to Cuba?" Uchenna asked.

Professor Fauna grinned at her mysteriously.

"Eyes on the sky, Professor," Uchenna reminded him.

He looked back out the window. The plane dipped violently again.

Elliot screamed, *"No!"*

"It's okay," Uchenna reassured him. "We're not crashing. Yet."

"It's not that," Elliot replied

"Then what?"

Elliot pointed at his shoes.

Jersey had thrown up all over them.

CHAPTER FOUR

Uchenna found a grease-stained rag behind their seats, and now Elliot was gingerly using it to get vomit off his shoes. Thankfully, Jersey was very small, so there was only a little bit. But it was still incredibly gross.

"It's very nutty," said Elliot.

"Everything we do with Professor Fauna is nutty," said Uchenna.

"I'm talking about the—" Elliot looked up from his shoes to see Uchenna grinning at him. "Oh," he said. "Very funny."

"It is probably because I feed him so many almond bars!" Professor Fauna added. Elliot's stomach lurched.

And then, Uchenna began to hum.

"No," said Elliot. "Not about this! Please . . ."

But Uchenna was already singing in the style of an old-fashioned crooner.

"The way to Cuba is bumpy,
And little Jersey is blue!
He throws up something quite lumpy
All over Elliot's shoes!"

Elliot was still scraping puke off his laces. "Can I just say that I *hated* that one?"

Uchenna snickered.

"Shall we return to the business at hand?" Professor Fauna said. He squinted into the bright clouds as the plane continued to dance. "This sea serpent is referred to as the *Madre de aguas*."

"The . . . Mother of Waters?" said Uchenna.

"*Muy bien*. They say that without the Madre de aguas, the Mother of Waters, there would be no fresh water anywhere in Cuba." Professor Fauna scoffed. "Now, to me, saying that the fresh water of an entire island depends on one creature sounds like magic. And, as you know, the creatures of myth and legend are *not* magic. They are creatures. *But* . . . they often have evolutionary mutations that can *seem* like magic."

"What evolutionary mutation could possibly control the fresh water of an entire island?" Elliot asked.

"I do not know. Perhaps it purifies the water by passing it through its gills? Or perhaps it draws the fresh water up from the aquifer somehow?"

Jersey was clawing at the compartment of the backpack where his almond bars were kept. "No!" Elliot said to him. "Under *no* circumstances, Jersey." Jersey began whining plaintively. "Not a *chance*, you little puke-Devil!"

Professor Fauna went on. "Many islands in

the Caribbean tell stories of the Madre de aguas, and she goes by many names and takes many forms. But of course, this makes sense. There are many different peoples in the Caribbean, so of course they would talk about the Madre de aguas in different ways! Anyway, in Cuba people all over the island used to talk of the enormous serpent living in their wells and their ponds, wherever there was fresh water. But lately fewer and fewer people have seen the Madre de aguas. It could be there were once many Madres de aguas in Cuba and only one survives today, or it could be that there was only ever one, moving between different bodies of water, but today she hides herself from all but a few human eyes. I do not know. What I *also* do not know is this: Where is the Madre de aguas of Cuba now? Rosa was one of the people who the Madre de aguas still visited, and she has not seen the serpent for some weeks."

Professor Fauna suddenly pointed through the windshield. "There!" he exclaimed. "The

Miami airport! This is where we are meeting Yoenis, Rosa's son."

Uchenna and Elliot looked out of the window. Peeking through heavy clouds were the runways and parking lots of a huge airport.

"Wait, you're going to land at an *airport*?" said Uchenna. "That's a first. We usually just plow into trees or a cliff or something."

"Do you have clearance to land at the Miami airport?" Elliot asked. "I'm pretty sure you need official permission or somethin—AHHH!"

A gigantic commercial passenger jet buzzed just above their heads. The *Phoenix* bobbed and weaved in the enormous power of the jet's wake. Professor Fauna wrestled with the plane's controls. Which seemed to do nothing. The plane dipped, nose down, toward the tarmac.

"Goodness gracious!" Elliot screamed.

The plane was screaming, too, the wind ripping past its wings.

And then, at the last second, the yoke finally

responded to Professor Fauna's entreaties, the plane leveled off, and the wheels touched down on the tarmac at a distant end of the runway, far from the main terminals and commercial jets.

They rolled to a stop.

"I think I am getting better at this!" Professor Fauna exclaimed

Jersey smiled at him. Then he put his little blue head between Elliot's legs.

"NO!" Elliot cried, and Jersey puked on his shoes again.

CHAPTER FIVE

Standing on the tarmac by a chain-link fence, at the very far end of the Miami airport runway, was a tall young man with thick black hair. He was surrounded by more than a dozen suitcases. He waved at the professor.

"Yoenis!" Professor Fauna cried. He looked back at Elliot and Uchenna. "This is our friend!"

"Uh . . . ," said Uchenna, staring out the window, "does he think those bags will all fit in the *Phoenix*?"

Elliot had returned to cleaning Jersey Devil vomit from his shoes. He looked up and out the window to see a man standing amidst an *island* of bags.

Professor Fauna stopped the plane, threw his door open, and hopped out. The warm, humid Florida air hit Uchenna. She clambered down and followed Professor Fauna over to the man with the suitcases.

"*¡Yoenis! ¿Qué tal estás?*"

Yoenis smiled and embraced the professor, and they kissed each other on one cheek. Then he

turned to Uchenna and Elliot. "These must be Elliot and Uchenna," he said, and shook both their hands very seriously. "I'm Yoenis."

Uchenna tried to smile at him, but she was distracted by *all the bags*. There were so many suitcases and bags around Yoenis's feet that she thought he must have disobeyed every public announcement ever made and agreed to watch the suitcases of every other passenger at the Miami airport. They *couldn't* all belong to him.

"I see you're looking at my luggage," Yoenis said. "I'll have to rearrange some things, but don't worry. It'll all fit."

"Um . . . I hope this isn't rude," said Uchenna, "but there is *no chance* that will all fit in the *Phoenix*."

"Even if it did, I'm pretty sure planes have weight limits," Elliot added. "For *safety*." He glanced back at the *Phoenix*, where Jersey was peeking through a small round window. He seemed to be staring at Yoenis's baggage, too.

"Don't worry about my stuff. Any Cuban who goes home knows how to pack a lot in a little space. I wish we didn't have to. But we do."

"Why?" Uchenna asked.

Yoenis bent over and started to open some of the bags. "Hold this open for me," Yoenis said, handing Elliot a large Ziploc and pouring a bottle of vitamins into it. "It's a long story. Basically, it's hard for Cubans to get all the things they need. The Cuban government makes it tough. And *then*, the US government goes and makes it even *harder* by imposing an embargo." While he was talking, Yoenis pulled out more vitamins, several bags of powdered milk, nuts, dried fruit, and a big box of dried soup.

"Between the Cuban and US governments, my mother can't get the basic things she needs to live. Milk, meat, medicine, machinery." Yoenis explained. "*Ya tú sabes.* Those in power are always making the lives of regular people miserable. Anyway, whenever a Cuban American goes back to Cuba to see his family, he pretty much always brings a few things."

Elliot gestured at the bags. "A *few* things?"

"My man," Yoenis chuckled darkly, "this is *nada*. You should see what I bring when I fly commercial."

Yoenis turned his focus to packing, and Uchenna started gazing around the Miami airport. Suddenly, she muttered, "Unbelievable!" She pointed to a large airplane hangar at the end of the runway. A large cargo plane was being loaded. The plane was silver, but the wings and tail were painted black, and on the tail was a snakelike *S*. Uchenna groaned. "They are *everywhere*."

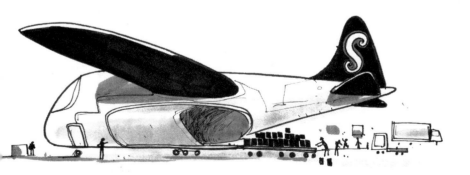

Elliot came next to her and shaded his eyes from the Miami sun. "Seriously. They take *multinational corporation* to a ridiculous extreme."

"Who's that?" Yoenis asked, shoving a pair of sneakers into a crevice about the size of a single sock.

Professor Fauna passed him another pair of sneakers, which Yoenis somehow shoved into the same space, and said, "The Schmoke Brothers. Billionaire industrialists. Collectors of mythical creatures. Villains of the lowest order."

"More powerful rich guys," Yoenis replied, "exploiting the world, its people, its animals, its resources. No surprise." Then he straightened up. "But someone was talking about these Schmokes recently . . . ," Yoenis said. He tapped his chin, trying to remember what he'd heard.

Elliot squinted. "Can you see what they're loading?"

"Looks like black barrels?" Uchenna said. "What do you think is in them?"

Elliot shrugged. "Pure evil, probably."

Yoenis laughed out loud at that. "Elliot, I like you." Elliot grinned. Then Yoenis stood up and dusted off his hands. Elliot and Uchenna looked around. Their mouths fell open. There was a single suitcase sitting at his feet.

"Are you kidding me?" Elliot exclaimed.

"What?" said Yoenis. "I told you that Cubans know how to pack."

"That thing must be dense as a black hole," Elliot said.

Yoenis shrugged and picked it up and hefted it toward the *Phoenix*. Professor Fauna held a door open for him, and he threw the bag in the back. "Next stop," announced the professor, "*¡Cubita la bella!*"

CHAPTER SIX

The clouds around Cuba were even darker and more intense than they had been in New Jersey. The *Phoenix* bounced and jerked through them. Jersey looked bluer than usual. Elliot stuck his finger in his little face. "Don't you dare . . ."

"It *really* looks like it's going to rain," Uchenna murmured, staring out the windows.

"It's looked like this for months," said Yoenis. "And it just *won't.*"

"The news says there's a twenty-five percent chance," Elliot told him.

"The Cuban weather reports have been saying *that* for months, too. If only it would. This drought is killing Cuba's crops, and the tourist hotels are limiting water for showers—if this goes on, we'll have no crops and no money from tourism. That means everyone's going to be starving."

Uchenna looked at Yoenis. "What you're saying is, we *have* to *find* the Madre de aguas."

"You said it, little sister."

Professor Fauna steered the *Phoenix* below the cloud line, and they began circling Havana, a dense city of tall buildings, built around a crescent bay and a wide river. Sunlight filtered through the low clouds.

"Looks a little like Heaven, doesn't it?" Yoenis said.

"I was just thinking that," agreed Uchenna.

"And it could be," Yoenis said. "If the people

were ever able to take power. But to more imme-
diate business: *¿Dónde vas a aterrizar, Profesor?*"

The professor was squinting down at the
busy, crowded city. "I don't know. I don't usually
make it to the point in the flight where we have
to *decide* to land."

"How about an airport?" said Elliot. "That
was a really nice change!"

Professor Fauna pointed to a wide stretch of
road right next to the bay. Waves crashed up on
black rocks, spraying pedestrians who were walking beside a stone seawall. "What about there?"

"That's the roadway along the seawall, the *malecón*," said Yoenis. "It's pretty busy, especially during the day. . . ."

But Professor Fauna was already aiming the *Phoenix* directly toward it.

"Um, Professor," said Yoenis. "This isn't a good idea."

Professor Fauna seemed not to be listening.

"Professor!" Uchenna tried to get his attention, too.

"Professor!" Elliot cried.

Horns were honking and people were yelling.

Professor Fauna's tongue was sticking out of his mouth. He was concentrating as hard as he could. The *malecón* was approaching fast.

Yoenis covered his eyes. Uchenna covered her eyes. Jersey climbed onto Elliot's face and covered his eyes for him.

Professor Fauna started screaming.

The wheels touched the roadway.

"I did it!" Professor Fauna screamed.

"*¡Así se hace!*" cried Yoenis. "Now slow down!"

But the *Phoenix* was not slowing down.

"Mito, use the brakes!"

"What brakes?!" Professor Fauna shouted.

The *Phoenix* hit the wall that ran between the roadway and Havana Bay. And suddenly, the *Phoenix* was spinning like a wheel, wing over wing. Everyone was screaming.

They hit the water. Hard.

CHAPTER SEVEN

"Out, out, out!" shouted Professor Fauna.

He pushed open the doors before they were submerged, and soon Uchenna, Elliot, Professor Fauna, and Yoenis were swimming in the water of Havana Bay.

"We're alive!" Uchenna crowed. She looked around. "Right? You're all alive?"

"I'm alive!" said Professor Fauna, treading water. "Yoenis, are you alive?"

Yoenis was holding on to a wing of the *Phoenix*. "I'm alive! Elliot, are you alive?"

Elliot burst up through the surface, coughing and spitting.

"He's alive!" Uchenna shouted. "But . . . where's Jersey?"

Just then, Jersey popped out of the water, too, in an eruption of red wings and tiny coughs. He flapped his away above the waves and then landed on Elliot's head. "Hey! Jersey! Come on, treading water is hard enough!"

"Ugh!" Uchenna spat. "Do *not* drink the water!"

"I wouldn't," said Yoenis, his head bobbing above the small waves. "Havana's waste gets dumped in the bay. Look—there's a sewage drain." He nodded at a small pipe that was protruding from the *malecón*. Dirty water was pouring out of it into the bay. Then Yoenis tried to climb up on the *Phoenix*'s wing. When his back was to the drain, a small creature stuck its head out of the pipe.

"What is *that*?" Uchenna exclaimed, kicking

hard with her legs to keep her head above the oily, fishy water.

"Looks like some kinda lizard?" said Elliot. "Or fish? Or footless amphibian? I can't tell from here." His head sunk beneath the surface of the water, and when he came back up, he was shouting, "Oh, the water is in my mouth! Oh, it's in my mouth, get it out!"

The little creature raised its head. It was blue-green, with a body like a snake's. It appeared to have ornate horns on its head. And even from a distance they could see its eyes—a shining midnight blue. Suddenly, it slid out of the sewage pipe

and slipped into the water of the bay, and then it was gone beneath the waves.

"What *was* that?" Uchenna said.

Yoenis, half up on the plane's wing, turned toward the sewage pipe again. "What was what?"

Professor Fauna was swimming around like he was enjoying himself. But Uchenna and Elliot were treading water and looking at one another. "That thing was *weird*," said Uchenna.

"Yeah," agreed Elliot. "That was definitely not any creature I'm familiar with. It looked like a snake crossed with a bull crossed with a—"

Just then, they felt the water vibrate below them. Which was a strange feeling, because water doesn't normally vibrate. Uchenna looked down and could just make out, through the murky water, the strange creature. It seemed to be swimming up, toward them, getting larger as it came. But not larger in the way that an object *usually* gets larger as it comes toward you. Larger at a *much* faster rate. Unnaturally fast. Like it was *growing*.

"Uh, Elliot?" said Uchenna.

"I see it, Uchenna!" Elliot replied. "Swim for your lives!"

They both started swimming toward the *Phoenix* as fast as they could.

There was a roar of water behind them.

Everyone was screaming.

CHAPTER EIGHT

Sharp horns pierced the surface of the water, and then a scaly head emerged, and finally two sparkling, midnight-blue eyes.

It was the same head and face they had seen in the sewage spout. But now it was *enormous*.

The creature rose up out of the water. Its neck and body were as wide as the base of a palm tree. It was a sea serpent—a humungous, terrifying sea serpent—and it rose in a coiling spiral until it towered above the members of the Unicorn Rescue Society.

"*Is that . . . ?*" Professor Fauna whispered, his voice a blend of fear and excitement.

"*That's the Madre de aguas,*" Yoenis whispered back. "*My mom's friend from her* fuentecita. *I knew she could change sizes, but I've never seen anything like this. . . .*"

The giant sea serpent gnashed her teeth, each one like a terrible fishhook, curving and sharp and large enough to hook a great white shark. The Madre de aguas's purple tongue twisted in the air.

And then she began to swim toward the *Phoenix . . .* which the members of the Unicorn Rescue Society were still clinging to desperately.

"This is bad," said Elliot.

"Is it bad?" Uchenna asked Yoenis. "Is she dangerous? Isn't she your friend?"

"I don't know. We used to hang out when she was in my mom's fountain. Maybe she'll remember me?"

Suddenly, the sea serpent pulled her head back. She looked like a snake about to strike.

"Okay," said Yoenis. "I'm with Elliot. This is bad."

The Madre de aguas roared, shaking the surface of the water—it looked like something right out of a nightmare.

She lunged.

And then, she . . . *squeaked.*

The sound she made could only be described as a squeak.

And she dove away, into the waves.

They all stared, completely confused as to why they were not dead.

Jersey swooped down toward the surface of the water. The Madre de aguas stuck her head out of the water, saw Jersey, and dove back under the waves. She was now hurrying away from them, getting smaller and smaller as she went, until she was invisible in the bright blue bay. They saw a splash as she leapt up and into the sewage pipe, small as she had been when they first saw her. And then she disappeared into the darkness.

"Wow." Uchenna was gazing at Jersey, who was flapping above the waves. "I think Jersey just scared off the Madre de aguas."

"I am inclined to agree with you," Professor Fauna said. "As difficult as that is to believe." The water was lapping the professor's soaked suit jacket, shirt, and tie.

Yoenis had clambered into the cockpit of the *Phoenix*. "I'm going to call for help," he said. "My cousin, Maceo, pilots a barge that cleans junk out of the bay. Maybe he can help with this plane."

"Are you calling the *Phoenix* junk?!" Professor

Fauna exclaimed, holding on to a wing of the *Phoenix*.

"*Exacto*, Mito," Yoenis replied. He fiddled with the two-way radio and then spoke into it. "*Limpiador, Limpiador, Limpiador para Phoenix. Cambio.*"

Some garbled speech came out of the radio, and Yoenis broke into a grin.

"*¡Hola, primo! ¡Sí, fui yo! ¡Ven a buscarnos! Cambio y fuera.*"

CHAPTER NINE

They were all warm and getting drier now, wrapped in thick blankets that Yoenis's cousin Maceo had given them. They stood on a barge called *El Limpiador de la Bahía*, the *Bay Cleaner*, as it steamed toward the *malecón*. Maceo had managed to fish the *Phoenix* out of the bay with a small crane that he used for salvaging junk. Usually, though, the junk that he saved didn't have people hanging off of it.

Professor Fauna had managed to retrieve all

the papers he'd brought from his office from the floor of the *Phoenix*. Maceo had given him a black trash bag and Professor Fauna hugged it to his chest.

Yoenis, with his one incredibly dense suitcase beside him, talked animatedly with Maceo, explaining what they had seen. Jersey shook himself and frolicked in the sunshine among the salvaged junk, jumping from a waterlogged sofa to an old crate to a black barrel. Maceo tried not to stare. Elliot was attempting to wring the bay water out of his grandmother's sweater. "I am so

amazingly dead." He sniffed the sweater. "Ugh! My mom is definitely going to want to know why this smells like oil and dead fish!"

"Hey, Elliot," said Uchenna. She was looking at the black barrel Jersey was now perched on. He was trying to clean his fur with his tongue, but kept having to stop to gag and spit out the filthy water.

"I'm not going near him," said Elliot. "He will *not* throw up on me again."

"No, not Jersey," said Uchenna. *"Look."*

She pointed to a silver snakelike *S* on the barrel.

"No," Elliot moaned. "Nooo. *Nooooooo."*

Professor Fauna heard Elliot's moaning. He came over. Uchenna said, "Professor, look." Her fingers traced small white letters that ran in along the curved edge of the barrel lid: SCHMOKE'S SURE-TO-CHOKE INSECTICIDE.

The professor sighed heavily. "So they are in Cuba, too? Hm. Well, if face them we must, then face them we will. But for now, we must gather information. Let us meet Rosa. And then, the library!"

"What?" said Uchenna. "The library?"

"The National Archives, to be exact!" Professor Fauna replied, cradling his black trash bag a little closer. "You see, this is the *third* reason we came to Cuba!"

"Because you wanted to go to the library?" Uchenna asked.

"I sympathize," Elliot added. "But we do have libraries in New Jersey."

"Ah, *amiguitos*, you do not understand. The third reason we came to Cuba is that . . . I am hot on the trail of . . . *the world's missing unicorns*!"

"What?" said Elliot. "Seriously?"

And Uchenna said, "That. Is. Awesome."

CHAPTER TEN

Yoenis led the members of the Unicorn Rescue Society off his cousin's barge and over the edge of the *malecón*. Professor Fauna turned and bid farewell to his airplane.

"I hope I see the *Phoenix* again," Professor Fauna sniffed.

"I don't," Elliot said.

"Don't worry, Mito," Yoenis reassured him. "You'll get your *avioncito* back. Maceo's other job is fixing old cars. Look around. Thanks to the embargo and terrible government policies, many of the cars in Havana are *seventy* years old. If Maceo can make a seventy-year-old car run like new, I think he can fix the *Phoenix*."

"Yeah, but the seventy-year-old cars don't crash every single time you drive them," Elliot objected.

"*Eso sí es cierto*," Yoenis agreed. "Well, we'll see what Maceo can do. Now come on, follow me."

Uchenna slipped Jersey into the backpack—luckily, the air holes and synthetic fabric meant that it was the least waterlogged thing they had—and they followed Yoenis. He waved back to Maceo on the barge, while the Professor blew kisses at the *Phoenix* with the hand that wasn't cradling the trash bag with his wet papers.

Yoenis led the group away from the water, back to the road that ran parallel to the *malecón*, snaking around the bay in the shape of a seashell. Beyond the street, a wall of buildings followed the same curve. To Elliot, the buildings seemed like city guards, hiding the city beyond from view. From where they stood, the structures looked as if they stood shoulder to shoulder, keeping everyone out. It was only when they crossed the street that Elliot saw the narrow roads between the buildings, leading deeper into the city.

"Come on," Yoenis said. "Let me show you my favorite part of Cuba: *La Habana vieja*—Old Havana."

Uchenna, Elliot, and Fauna followed Yoenis through one of the gaps between the buildings, onto a narrow, potholed road, shaded by buildings with elaborate moldings and intricate carvings. Some of the buildings were painted bold colors—pinks and purples and teals and yellows, so bright that Elliot thought they belonged in a storybook. But other buildings looked as if they were being devoured from the outside in: Gray cement bubbled through fading, peeling paint; steel rebar stuck out like broken bones from crumbling facades. Most of the buildings, beautiful and decrepit alike, had iron balconies with spirals and curlicues. Dozens of electrical wires crisscrossed above their heads. They looked just as decorative as the balconies.

"Havana used to be one of the ritziest cities in the world," Yoenis said. "The newest music, dance, poetry; global businesses and world famous entertainment."

Uchenna and Elliot looked around at the

colorful, beautiful, shabby city. It was marvelous. It did *not* look ritzy.

"But all of that glamour and success—it was only for the rich. For years, the Cuban people tried to choose their own government, to have control over the beauty and resources of Cuba. And for years, powerful outsiders held us down. When Columbus first arrived in Cuba, he said it was the most beautiful place on earth, claimed it for Spain, and then he started killing the Taíno, the Native People who live here."

Down an alleyway, there was shouting. Some children, boys and girls, their skin all different colors, played baseball with a stick and tattered ball. They were laughing and yelling at each other.

Yoenis smiled and then went on. "Enslaved people were brought here in chains from Africa, kidnapped to work in brutal conditions growing sugar and other crops. It's always the same story— some people have power, and they make everyone else suffer. Finally, at the turn of the twentieth century, the people of Cuba overthrew the Spanish rulers—"

"That sounds good!" said Uchenna.

"Yeah, it was good. For about a minute," Yoenis replied. "And then big American businesses came and decided that Cuba was a place to make money—for big American businesses. They chose our leaders. They chose our laws. And they left most Cubans desperately poor. As we like to say, *'Se quedaron con la quinta y con los mangos.'* Which means, roughly, 'They took the farmhouse and all the mangoes, too.'"

Yoenis stooped down and picked up an empty bottle of dish soap. An old woman poked her head out of the door and motioned with her hand. He brought it to her, and she smiled.

"And then, there was one last revolution. The Cuban people had a dream that all money would be shared. And that we would all decide our fate together, through truly free elections. So the rich were overthrown, the big American businesses kicked out, and a communist government was founded."

"Was *that* good?" Elliot asked.

Yoenis snorted. "What do *you* think? The Communists collected everyone's money . . . and then forgot to share it. Or, to be fair, did a bad job of it. And the US imposed the embargo, to punish us for kicking out the big American businesses. So we can't get new cars or materials to repair our buildings. Every year, we grow poorer. The Communists ended freedom of speech, so if you complain too loudly, you can end up in jail. And we haven't had a real election since they took over."

Yoenis led them onto a beautiful little street, where the houses were better maintained, and an older man was telling a story—above their heads. He was sitting on his balcony, and other older folks were sitting on theirs, laughing across the street at the tale he told.

"And that's the history of Cuba so far," said

Yoenis. "But this is not the end. What will happen next? Will Cuba be for the powerful, or for the people?" He looked at Uchenna, Elliot, and Professor Fauna. "Maybe, together, we can write a happier chapter."

Uchenna said, "Yoenis, whatever we can do, we will."

He gave her a half smile. "You know what, Uchenna? For the first time in a long time, you give me a little bit of hope."

CHAPTER ELEVEN

They jumped over a puddle of mud and passed a stray dog sprawled out on the sidewalk with his tongue hanging out, trying to get cool. Elliot wished he could cool himself like that—the sun, the humid air, the smell of diesel and salt was wearing him out.

"WHAT?" Yoenis said. "They have got to be kidding."

The members of the Unicorn Rescue Society found themselves gazing across a plaza. Wide stones reflected the bright sunshine. Royal palms formed a square in the center of the plaza.

It should have been beautiful.

But one side of the plaza was dominated by a gleaming marble building with sparkling glass windows that seemed completely out of place in Old Havana.

"A new hotel," Professor Fauna said.

"A new hotel is one thing," Yoenis said. "But this isn't just any new hotel. Read the sign."

Elliot read the words engraved in gold across the front of the hotel:

SCHMOKE INTERNATIONAL HOTEL

A PROJECT OF SCHMOKE HOSPITALITY GROUP

Treating You the Way You Deserve

"*¡Hermanos del diablo!*" Professor Fauna spat.

"I don't know what the professor just said," Elliot muttered. "But I think I agree."

Uchenna marched across the square and

pressed her face against a window of the new hotel.

"Uchenna!" Elliot hissed, coming up behind her. He looked around nervously. "What if they see us?"

"Whoa, it's like a palace in there," Uchenna said, ignoring Elliot. "There's a fountain in the lobby that's bigger than my house. And it's *made of gold*."

Elliot looked around a few more times to ensure that the Schmoke Brothers themselves hadn't suddenly appeared in Cuba. Then he peered inside, too. After a moment, he said, "It

looks like they're preparing for some kind of banquet." All around the soaring lobby, waiters in black bow ties were running around setting up tables and throwing elegant white tablecloths over them. There was a large, strangely shaped golden fountain in the middle of the room. From outside the hotel, they couldn't make out what it was supposed to be.

Elliot watched as two of the waiters stood on ladders and unfurled a banner. The banner read, *Bienvenidos, capitanes de agricultura.* And below it, in English: *Welcome, Captains of Agriculture!*

"Captains of Agriculture?" Uchenna repeated. "What does that mean?"

"Uh, agriculture is farming . . . so really good farmers, I guess?" Elliot answered.

Uchenna said, "Aren't the Schmokes more like the type of people who invite, I don't know, *royalty* to their parties?"

Yoenis had come up behind them. "Could

be farmers," he said, putting his face against the window, too. "Or could be the government officials in charge the Cuban farming industry. Either way, something smells fishy," he agreed.

Elliot looked down at himself. "It may be my sweater."

Yoenis surveyed the scene for another moment, and then he said, "Well, if anyone knows what's going on, it's my mother. *Vengan.* Her house isn't far from here."

CHAPTER TWELVE

The group walked under a blue sky criss-crossed with low-hanging electrical wires and between apartment buildings that seemed to lean over the narrow streets. Yoenis came to a stop in front of a bright yellow building with a large brown door. He knocked loudly. *"¡Mamá!"* he called.

A French window opened above them, and a small woman with short hair burst out onto a small balcony. She had brown, wrinkled skin, muscular arms, and light gray eyes. *"¡Mi'jito!"* she shouted, and fled the balcony. A moment later, the front door was thrown open and the little woman burst through it and wrapped her arms around Yoenis's neck. She hung on to him for a long time. Yoenis laughed and tried to stand up, but she wouldn't let go so he lifted her with him. Then they were both laughing. She let go and dropped to her feet, then turned to the children.

"Bienvenidos a La Habana. Me llamo Rosa. Come in, please."

They followed Rosa through the door and into her home. Except, they weren't actually inside. They were standing in a small courtyard, lush with plants and a little fountain in the center. The walls surrounding the courtyard were painted the same yellow as the exterior of Rosa's house. Windows looked down into the verdant space.

"Whoa . . . ," Uchenna breathed. "This is *beautiful.*"

Big fronded plants reflected the sun that shone down into the courtyard. There was a little waterfall that tumbled from a rock sculpture into the fountain. A small tree with gray bark stood behind the fountain.

Jersey, in the backpack on Uchenna's back, started to wriggle. Rosa pointed and said, "*Déjalo*. Let him out." So Uchenna put the backpack on her stomach and unzipped it. Jersey poked his head out and started sniffing the air. Rosa laughed. Yoenis laughed seeing his mother laugh. Then Jersey bounded out of the bag and into the garden, where he started to frolic under the plants.

"Jersey, come back!" Elliot called.

But Rosa said, "*Shh*. Let him play." She turned to Professor Fauna. "Erasmo, thank you for coming. Please, put down your trash bag."

Fauna put down his bag of papers on a chair, and Rosa grasped both of his hands in hers and looked him in the eyes. He smiled. He introduced

Elliot and Uchenna. Then he nodded at Jersey, who was running and leaping and then rolling on his back at their feet.

"He is very happy here," said the professor.

"He knows that it is a special place." Rosa turned to Elliot and Uchenna. "Children," she said. "It is nice to meet you. Now come, I have something to show you."

So they followed Rosa to the tree with the smooth gray bark.

"This is a ceiba tree. Have you ever seen one before?"

Uchenna and Elliot shook their heads.

"For thousands of years, ceiba trees have been important to the people of Cuba." Rosa rubbed her wrinkled hand up and down the trunk. "Go ahead," she said.

The children rubbed the tree. It felt almost . . . soft.

Rosa said, "The ceiba is sacred to the Taíno, the Native People of this island. Then, the first thing the Spanish did when they invaded Cuba in 1519 was gather under a great ceiba tree and pray, to give thanks for arriving safely in this land. And, not much later, when Europeans began enslaving people in Africa and bringing them across the Atlantic, those people sought out their holy tree, the baobab tree—but those West African trees don't grow here. The ceiba tree looks a little like the baobab, though, and so the ceiba became the holy tree of Afro-Cubans as well."

Rosa looked from Uchenna to Elliot to Professor Fauna, to make sure they were all listening carefully. They were. "This tree is like Cuba. We are many peoples. Some have always lived here. But over time, we have grown together. Our belief systems have merged, separated, overlapped—just like our music, our dance, our food. Like many roots feeding one tree, drawing water from distant sources. The ceiba tree is Cuba's people and Cuba itself."

The members of the Unicorn Rescue Society nodded solemnly.

"I told you my mother and I see the history of Cuba differently," Yoenis told them.

"Ah," Rosa said, shaking her head, "did you lecture them on politics already? *Mi pobre gente*, Yoenis can go *on* and *on*."

"*¡Mamá!*" Yoenis exclaimed, half laughing, half exasperated. "*You* just lectured them for ten minutes! And your silly 'we are one Cuba' story is a nice dream, but the more important story is how power has been stolen from the people!"

"The people will only regain their power," Rosa said, "by relying on the many histories and cultures of Cuba."

"*Mamá*, that makes no—"

"I am sorry to interrupt," Professor Fauna interjected, putting an arm around the old woman, "but I get the sense that you two have had this argument before?"

"It's been going on for the last twenty years or so," Rosa admitted.

"Then I don't think you will solve it now. Whereas the problem of the Madre de aguas . . ."

"Yes!" Rosa agreed. "*¡La pobrecita!* My sweet, little lost friend!"

Elliot said, "Um, I don't mean to be rude, but based on some recent field observations I've made, the Madre de aguas is not lost. Or little. Or sweet."

"Field observations?" Rosa was confused. "*Pero*, when?"

"Just now in the bay," Uchenna replied.

"When she tried to eat us," said Elliot.

CHAPTER THIRTEEN

"¿*Q*ué dicen?" Rosa exclaimed. "*¿Mi amiga intentó comérselos?*"

"*Sí, Mamá.* We've had quite an adventure already," Yoenis told her. "Maybe we can get cleaned up, eat a little, and tell you what happened?"

"Absolutely not!" Rosa replied, to everyone's surprise. Then she added. "You will eat *a lot!*"

A few minutes later, they were all sitting in Rosa's kitchen. The furniture was very spare, but the yellow walls and the delicious smell made the kitchen cozy and welcoming. Rosa stood on a step stool and stirred something in a big black pot. She and Jersey had already become fast friends. He was perched on her shoulder, staring into the pot. Rosa didn't seem to mind.

"It smells amazing," said Uchenna. Her stomach gurgled.

"*Ropa vieja*," Rosa replied, without turning around.

"Translates as 'old clothes,'" Yoenis informed them.

Elliot said, "Really? Uh, I'm not *that* hungry. . . ." And then he added, under his breath, "I mean, I knew things under the embargo were tough, but old clothes?"

Yoenis threw his head back and laughed. "We just *call* it that. It's strips of beef.

Kinda *looks* like boiled shredded up old clothes, though. It's a real specialty. These days, finding *ropa vieja* outside of a hotel is almost impossible. But my mother knew we were coming, and so she spent *way* too much money, and I'm sure she spent three hours on line at the store—"

"Tsk! Tsk! Tsk! No more of that," Rosa scolded him. She put down a plate of *ropa vieja* in front of Elliot.

Soon, they were all digging into the most delicious old clothes Elliot and Uchenna had ever tasted. Rosa even made a bowl for Jersey and put it on the floor. He buried his little face in it. They heard noisy, wet slurping.

"Jersey!" said Uchenna. "Manners!"

But Elliot tapped her on the shoulder and pointed at Professor Fauna. Professor Fauna's face was also buried in his *ropa vieja*. *He* was the one making the disgusting slurping sounds.

"*Ahora,*" said Rosa, after everyone had

finished their second helpings. "*Cuéntenme*. You saw my friend?"

So Yoenis and the members of the URS told Rosa about their terrifying—and confusing—encounter with the Madre de aguas.

Rosa chuckled through the whole story. "*Bueno*," she said when they'd finished. "She *is* feisty. Good you had your brave little defender here." She rubbed Jersey's furry blue head. He looked up at her from his bowl, which he'd just licked clean. Rosa took her plate, which still had some *ropa vieja* on it, and put it on the floor.

"But clearly," Rosa went on, "something is wrong with the Madre de aguas. She was always feisty, but to charge across the bay to attack you? That is not right. And as long as something is wrong with her, the people of Cuba will continue suffering."

"More than normal," added Yoenis.

"As will the Madre de aguas!" Professor

Fauna exclaimed. "Let us not always be valuing *people* over *creatures*!"

"*Bien dicho*, Mito," Rosa said.

Elliot asked, "Can whatever is happening to the Madre de aguas *really* be causing this drought, though?" He gestured to the small window. "If those clouds just break, won't the drought be over? And what does a water serpent—even one with amazing abilities of expansion and contraction—have to do with whether it rains?"

Rosa said, "I don't pretend to understand it.

But in Cuba there are many beliefs about water, and my friend the Madre de aguas—"

"For the record she's the *only* one who calls her a 'friend'—"

"Yoenis, shush," Rosa said. "Just like the ceiba tree is revered by many different people in many different ways, so is the Madre de aguas. Some say she lives in salt water while others say in fresh water. In some countries she is like a mermaid, and in others she is a goddess. Some are afraid of her: There are stories of the Madre de aguas appearing as a ferocious sea monster as she did to you. But that is not the Madre de aguas I know. I believe if we are kind to our Madre de aguas, she is kind to us and brings us water."

"What was that you said about a goddess?" Uchenna asked, interested.

Rosa turned to Uchenna. "Not all Cubans believe that a sea serpent controls the waters. Many associate salt water with a goddess called Yemayá, and fresh water with a goddess called

Oshún. When the Yoruba people, from what we now call Nigeria, were enslaved and brought to Cuba by force, they brought Yemayá and Oshún with them."

"Wait, isn't your mom Nigerian?" Elliot asked Uchenna.

"Yeah, but we're not Yoruba. We're Igbo. Different peoples."

Elliot nodded and turned back to Rosa.

"There is another story," Rosa went on, "about María, the mother of Jesus, saving Cuban fishermen from drowning. When there is a drought, many Cubans pray to María, and she keeps them safe."

"Okay, I'm confused," Uchenna huffed. "Who should we be worrying about? The Madre de aguas? Or Oshún? Or Mary? Or Elliot's statistics?"

Rosa shrugged. "Mary. Oshún. Yemayá. The Madre de aguas. To me? Many roots. One tree."

"But can the Madre de aguas really control

the water?" Elliot demanded, wanting to get back to the science of it all. "That seems *really* hard to believe."

"Personally, I do not see how she could," Professor Fauna said. "That seems an evolutionary mutation too far."

Rosa said, "Well, there is one way to find out. Find her, help her, and let us see if this *sequía* ends."

"That," said Professor Fauna, "is a promise. But first, we have to make a quick stop at the Archives."

"The Archives?" Rosa said, surprised. "*¿Pero, por qué?*"

"*¡Busco un unicornio!*"

"What?!" Rosa exclaimed. "You seek a unicorn? In a library?"

But Professor Fauna had already marched, head held high and shoulders thrown back, out of the kitchen and toward the front door.

"Does he have any idea where the Archives are?" Yoenis wondered aloud.

Then, from the garden, they heard Professor Fauna call, "I just realized: I have no idea where the Archives are!"

Yoenis laughed and rolled his eyes. "I'll show him."

CHAPTER FOURTEEN

Yoenis led the professor, Uchenna, and Elliot through the narrow streets of Old Havana. They'd left Jersey to play in the garden, and Rosa sitting on an old wooden chair, watching him and throwing her head back with laughter.

As they left the house, Yoenis told them, "I have to stop in and see some friends around town. I'll let you look for your unicorn and meet you back at my mom's. You're sure you'll be able to find your way back?"

Elliot waved a hand at him. "Please. I once got lost in a shopping mall. It was awful. The worst three minutes of my life. I've never been lost since. I'll just memorize the route we take."

Yoenis looked at Uchenna. "Is he a little weird?"

"More than a little," Uchenna replied. "But he's the best adventuring buddy a kid could have."

Yoenis rubbed Elliot's curly hair. "I believe it."

They turned from one shady, potholed street into another, and then they emerged into an open plaza. But this one did not contain a sparkling, modern hotel. Instead, shading the plaza was the bell tower of an old monastery. The monastery was topped with red terra-cotta tile, and the walls were made of a warm, sand-colored stone. In the center of the plaza, a fountain encircled by four stone lions gurgled merrily. A band played a syncopated rhythm with guitars, bongos, and an instrument that looked something like a wooden gourd.

"What's that?" Uchenna pointed to the instrument as the musician ran a stick over the ridges on its front. She couldn't help tapping her feet as they played—the instrument looked like fun.

"That's a *güiro*," Yoenis said. "It's a Taíno instrument. And yet the rhythms that are making your feet tap uncontrollably are African rhythms. And the guitars are Spanish. This, *mi gente*, is what my mother was talking about. The combining of all of these traditions."

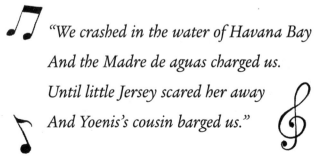

Uchenna spun in a circle, moving her shoulders from side to side. And then she burst into song, giving lyrics to the infectious melody:

"We crashed in the water of Havana Bay
And the Madre de aguas charged us.
Until little Jersey scared her away
And Yoenis's cousin barged us."

Yoenis threw his head back and laughed. They danced their way across the plaza. Finally, Yoenis led them into one of the side streets, and the rhythm of the band faded behind them.

Uchenna sighed happily. "I think I am in love with Cuba. Why did you ever leave, Yoenis? You seem so much happier here."

Yoenis's smile faded, and immediately Uchenna regretted the question. "I—" she stammered, "I—I'm sorry. That was a nosy question. I shouldn't have asked."

Yoenis sighed. "It's okay, Uchenna. It's a perfectly reasonable question. I'll tell you. The early 1990s were a really hard time for Cuba.

We'd gotten a lot of support from the Soviet Union. But when the Soviet Union fell apart, all of the food and aid they sent ended. It was a horrible time. People were starving. So they started making rafts. Rafts out of trash, rafts out of tires, rafts out of driftwood. Whatever they could find. And they'd try to ride the raft the ninety miles across the ocean to Florida."

"Whoa," said Uchenna. "That is incredibly brave."

"And *incredibly* dangerous!" Elliot added.

"You have no idea," Yoenis agreed. "My dad wanted to go with the rafters and

take me with him. He kept pointing out that he and my mother couldn't even feed me three meals a day. How hungry we were. My mother, she wanted to stay. She had a job working for the Cuban government, recording Cuba's cultural history. They had many fights. It was horrible."

Yoenis's face had become as dark as the clouds overhead. But like the clouds, no droplets fell.

"Finally, my dad convinced my mom that he and I should go. I don't know how. But I do remember my last day at our house. I spent it with the Madre de aguas."

"Really?" Professor Fauna asked.

"Yes. I was ten years old. I remember walking slowly around the garden, saying a silent good-bye to each plant, to the tiles, to the pavement stones. I tried to catch one last glimpse of the tiny hummingbird, the *zunzún*, that sometimes stopped by to visit. I was slowly sipping a can of cola that Mami had given me, trying to savor every last drop. It was a special treat for a very sad day.

"Then my dad called me from inside. *'Ya es hora.'*

"I turned back to the fountain. I wanted one last glimpse of the Madre de aguas, before I left. I wasn't sure if I'd ever see her again. *Please come,* I remember thinking. *Just one good-bye.*

"I leaned over the fountain. The shadows stirred. Something dark and shimmery stirred.

"And there she was.

"She swam up from the shadows at the bottom, her tiny horns just pricking the surface of the water.

"I laughed, and she began to puff up and grow, like a balloon inflating. As she did, the water levels in the fountain went down. Then, she shrank again, and the water rose once more."

Yoenis pursed his lips. In the momentary pause, Elliot said, "So, do you think she sucks up the water in order to grow? Like, through her scales or gills or something?"

Yoenis nodded. "Maybe," he said.

Uchenna nudged Elliot. "Let him tell the story."

"Right!" said Elliot. "Sorry. Science distracts me sometimes."

Yoenis smiled. "No worries. Once she was little again, I asked the Madre de aguas to take care of my mom. Through the food shortages and the power outages. To look after her. And just as I finished asking this of the Madre de aguas, my dad called me again. Loudly. I jumped. And I spilled my can of cola into the fountain. The dark cola bubbled and spread through the water.

"Suddenly the Madre de aguas was growing large again, larger than before. Her scales gleamed. She raised her body out of the water, rising like a corkscrew. Soon, she was towering over me, and there was no water in the fountain at all.

"I'd never seen her get so angry, and I hadn't seen her angry since, until today. So I apologized about a hundred times in one minute, and sopped up the cola from the lip of the fountain with my shirt. She calmed down, and shrank again, and the water rose. And the cola was gone—the water was totally clean."

"I'm sorry," Elliot said, "but I *have* to interrupt now. That may be how she provides fresh water to the islands—she purifies it by taking it in and letting it out again!"

"Maybe," Yoenis agreed. "Though that would mean the impurities remain inside of her."

"Which might put her in a really bad mood when there are a lot of impurities!" Elliot exclaimed.

"This is an excellent theory!" Professor Fauna agreed. "We shall have to write something up for the next issue of the *Journal of the Proceedings of the Unicorn Rescue Society*, Elliot!"

But Uchenna turned back to Yoenis. "So, you took a raft to Miami? Was it hard? Scary?"

"It was the worst," Yoenis said. "We made it, but barely. And that journey tore my family apart forever. My dad passed away a few years ago. He never made it back to Cuba."

Uchenna reached out her hand. Yoenis took it. They walked together, in silence, through the streets of Havana.

CHAPTER FIFTEEN

Yoenis soon brought them to a wide boulevard lined with royal palm trees. They stopped in front of a tall cream-colored colonial-style building. He shook hands with them all, gave Uchenna an extra wink to thank her for her kindness, and made absolutely certain that Elliot knew the way back to Rosa's.

After Yoenis had gone, Professor Fauna stood, staring up at the grand facade, a satisfied smile on his face, and his black trash bag clutched to

his chest. *"¡Miren, amiguitos!"* he said. *"¡El Archivo Nacional de la República de Cuba! Vengan,* let us see what treasures lie within!"

Professor Fauna led Elliot and Uchenna through the large gate, up some stairs, through a big wooden door, and into a grand foyer. The children looked around. The foyer was strangely empty. The only person there was a heavyset, grey-haired woman sitting at a tiny wooden desk by the door, reading a newspaper. She did not look up when they came in.

Professor Fauna approached her and gave a

small bow. *"Buenas, señora. ¿Dónde está el tarjetero, por favor?"*

Without looking up, the woman pointed across the foyer.

The members of the Unicorn Rescue Society walked into a high-ceilinged room with large open windows. One half of the room had long, shiny wooden tables, where people were quietly reading. The other half of the room was lined with rows and rows of huge wooden cabinets. Each wooden cabinet had dozens of tiny drawers.

"What in the world are those?" Uchenna asked. "Does this place keep the smallest books in the world in those drawers? Books for mice?"

But Elliot's eyes lit up. "No!" he exclaimed. "Those—Those are *card catalogs*!"

"What?" Uchenna asked, but Elliot was already rushing toward them. Uchenna followed. Meanwhile, Professor Fauna walked over to a counter built into a wall, where another woman read a newspaper.

Uchenna peered over Elliot's shoulder as he pulled open a tiny drawer. "Look!" he breathed. It was filled with thousands of yellowing index cards. Elliot picked one up. It was musty and brown at the corners, and it smelled a little.

"What *are* they?" Uchenna asked.

"Each card represents a book or a document. This is how libraries worked before computers. The cards are organized by subject, author, or title—depending on the drawer." He read the card he was holding:

"The author is José Martí. And the book is called *Documentos personales*. Unless this is just some documents. I can't tell. Ma456.78 is where on the shelf the librarian would find it." Elliot exhaled. "*So* cool."

Uchenna shrugged. Then she saw that Professor Fauna was struggling to get the woman at the counter to understand him.

In the little room behind the counter, smiling calmly and staring into the distance, was a very old man. Uchenna noticed that the man's eyes were milky blue. She wondered if he wasn't staring at anything at all—maybe he was blind.

Professor Fauna's voice was getting louder and louder. "*¡Se llama La Orden Secreta del Unicornio! ¡Debe de haber un expediente entero! ¡Con muchos documentos! ¡Un salón entero! ¿La Orden Secreta del Unicornio? ¿No? ¿Nada? ¿Segura? ¿Ni conoce La Orden? ¡Imposible! ¡No puede ser! ¡NO LO CREO!*"

At last Professor Fauna threw up his hands

and turned to Uchenna. "She has never *heard* of the Secret Order of the Unicorn!"

"Uh . . . ," said Uchenna, "neither have I."

"Yes, but you are not the guardian of their records! I am certain they are here! I have pieced together all the clues! Followed every lead! The records of the Secret Order of the Unicorn are—*there!*" He suddenly pointed. "The card catalog! That will tell me where they are!"

He hustled over. Uchenna watched him go. Then, to the lady behind the counter, who was reaching for her newspaper and looking completely unconcerned about never having heard of the Secret Order of the Unicorn, Uchenna said, "*¿El baño, por favor?*" The woman smiled at Uchenna and pointed back to the foyer.

Uchenna found the bathroom and went into a stall. When she was finished, she stood up and flushed.

And she screamed.

A huge blob of pink sludge was coming up through the toilet. She banged the door open and threw herself out of the stall. Uchenna turned and stared at the sludge bubbling up in the toilet bowl. She went to the sink and turned on the tap. Water. Not pink sludge. She washed her hands, and then went back to the toilet to see if she'd been imagining things.

She had not.

Pink sludge sat in the toilet. Suddenly, a bubble burst on its surface, sending a small eruption of sludge all over the walls of the stall. Uchenna was a brave girl, but she screamed again when that happened.

She hurried back to the reading room.

Professor Fauna and Elliot were hunched over two different tiny drawers, a few feet apart, whispering urgently.

"I have *secreción*, which means secretion. That's not right," Professor Fauna was saying. "I have *secretaria*, and *secular*, and *seco*. But no 'secret'!"

"And I have *ungüentos, uniformes militares, universos* . . . no 'unicorn'!" Elliot replied.

"*¡Mala palabra!*"

"Hey, you two," Uchenna interrupted them. "Something just happened in the bathroom."

Elliot and Professor Fauna kept up their frantic flipping through the musty catalog cards.

"Hey!"

"Next," Professor Fauna muttered, "we will check *orden*, or *sociedad*, or—"

Uchenna grabbed Elliot and spun him around. He stared at her. After a moment, he said, "What?"

And Uchenna replied, "You have to come to the girls' bathroom with me. Now."

CHAPTER SIXTEEN

Uchenna and Elliot peered down at the bubbly pink slime in the toilet.

"Gross," said Elliot.

"Yeah," agreed Uchenna. Then she added, "I don't know if it's related to what's happening to the Madre de aguas, but it *could* be."

Elliot stared at the pink sludge a moment longer. "Okay," he said. "Let's show the professor."

Back in the reading room, Professor Fauna had laid out all of his papers on one end of a long table.

Elliot rushed over to him. "Did you find the right card?"

"Perhaps! Perhaps!" the professor said. "I found a card that reads, 'Social Club of the Spanish Court—The Unicorns.' I have never heard of such a thing. But perhaps—"

"I don't have to remind you, Professor," said Elliot, "that you're not looking for a social club! You're looking for *actual* unicorns."

"Indeed! But the road to knowledge is long and winding, and sometimes we must follow it in unexpected directions."

"Elliot!" said Uchenna.

"*Shhh!*" A professorial woman at the other side of the table looked up from a large book and shushed them.

"*¡Perdón!*" Professor Fauna said, very loudly.

"*Shhhhhh!*" said a table full of professor-types all at once.

"*¡Perdón!*" Professor Fauna whispered back.

"*Professor Fauna!*" Uchenna hissed. "There is pink sludge in the ladies' toilet!"

"Ah!" he said. "Is there? Well, I don't know much about ladies' toilets. Is this normal?"

"No! Ugh!" Uchenna threw up her hands.

Just then, the woman from behind the desk walked up to them. She handed Professor Fauna a slip of paper. He held it up.

"What?!" Professor Fauna exclaimed.

"Shhh!" said all the other readers.

"What?!" he said again, but whispering this time. *"¿No están? Pero entonces, ¿dónde están?"*

"No sé," said the woman, and she walked back to her counter and her newspaper.

Professor Fauna hurried after her.

"What is going on?" Elliot asked.

Uchenna replied, "Well, I'm not exactly sure . . . but I think the papers Professor Fauna is looking for are missing."

CHAPTER SEVENTEEN

Professor Fauna was speaking urgently in Spanish to the woman who had resumed her spot behind the counter.

"*¿Pero cómo me puede decir que no están? Si antes me dijo que sí estaban—y ahora, ¿no están? ¿Cómo puede ser?*"

"*No sé.*"

Elliot tugged on Professor Fauna's jacket. "What did you say?"

Professor Fauna, as exasperated as they'd

ever seen him, turned to the children and said, "I asked, 'What do you *mean* the papers are not there? You are saying they were there, they have been there, but now they are not there? How can that happen?!'"

"And what did she say?"

"She said, 'I don't know'!" Professor Fauna turned back to the woman. *"¿Cuándo desaparecieron los papeles?"*

"No sé."

Elliot tugged on the professor's jacket again. "What did you ask her this time?"

"I asked her when the papers went missing."

"And what did she say?"

"Again, she does not know!" The professor turned to the woman again. *"Pero, ¿dónde podrían estar ahora?"*

"No sé."

Without waiting for Elliot to tug on his jacket, the professor turned to the kids and said, "I asked her where the papers could have gone. And she said—"

"Yeah, we got it," Uchenna interrupted. "*No sé.* She doesn't know." Then Uchenna said, "Maybe you should ask her who *does* know."

Professor Fauna cocked an eyebrow at Uchenna. "Huh," he said. "Good idea." He turned to the woman yet again. "*Y, ¿quién sí sabe?*"

The woman stared at Professor Fauna for a moment. Then she pointed behind her. "Juanito."

She was pointing at the old man with the milky eyes. He was still staring into the distance, smiling gently.

"*¿Puedo hablar con Juanito?*" Professor Fauna asked. And then, to the kids, he whispered, "*I asked to talk to Juanito.*"

The woman frowned, sighed, and finally shrugged. She walked over to the old man—Juanito—and spoke a few words in his ear. He seemed delighted to be spoken to, and he nodded eagerly. The woman glared at Professor Fauna, as if he'd started some kind of trouble. Then she slid an arm under Juanito's arm, put another arm around his back, and hoisted him to his feet.

With her help, Juanito shuffled over to the counter. He lay his hands on it, as if to steady himself. His hands were brown and the skin was so thin his veins looked like tree roots. Juanito smiled at them.

"*¿Cómo puedo ayudar?*"

Professor Fauna started to speak in Spanish. Slowly at first. Juanito nodded as he listened. As Juanito kept nodding, Professor Fauna began to go faster and faster, and to become more and more excited. Finally, the professor stopped. He leaned over the counter, bringing his nose almost in contact with Juanito's. And he said, "*Y, ¿entonces?*"

Juanito exhaled deeply. He shrugged. And he said, "*Yo conozco esos papeles.*"

"You do?!" Professor Fauna exclaimed in English. He turned to Elliot and Uchenna. "He knows them!"

"*Pero no están aquí.*"

"They are gone?!" Professor Fauna exclaimed, still in English. He turned to the kids. "They are—"

"Yeah," said Uchenna. "We heard you."

Juanito shrugged again. "*Me acuerdo de lo que decían . . .*"

Professor Fauna's mouth fell open.

"What?" Elliot asked, tugging on the professor's jacket again. "What'd he say?"

Professor Fauna translated: "He remembers what they said."

And so, in slow, careful Spanish, Juanito told Professor Fauna what the papers said.

CHAPTER EIGHTEEN

Professor Fauna walked through the streets of Old Havana with his black plastic bag cradled to his chest. He was walking slowly, beaming, like he was sleepwalking during a wonderful dream.

"Professor," said Elliot. "Professor! What did Juanito say?"

The professor shook himself from his daze. "What? Oh, I will tell you, children. I will tell you.

But first, we have a Madre de aguas to save!" He thrust a bony finger in the air.

"You're not going to tell us?!" Elliot exclaimed. "After all that?!"

"Patience, my young friend. Patience. We are not here on the trail of unicorns. We are here to help a majestic creature who is mysteriously suffering!" Elliot rolled his eyes and looked at Uchenna, who rolled her eyes right back. The professor didn't notice. "Now, let us talk about that disgusting pink sludge in the ladies' toi—"

HONNNNNNNK!

The members of the Unicorn Rescue Society jumped a foot in the air and spun around. A huge truck was trying to drive down the narrow street where they were walking. To get out of its way, they had to press themselves against the bright pink wall of a building.

The truck crawled past, belching hot fumes all over them.

When it had finally gone, they scraped themselves off the wall and tested if the air was safe to breathe again. Uchenna scowled after the truck. But her scowl turned into a disbelieving stare.

"Look!"

Elliot and the professor looked.

The truck was loaded with black barrels, each one emblazoned with a snakelike *S*.

At the very same instant, all three of them exclaimed, "Follow that truck!"

Because the streets of Old Havana were so narrow, the truck couldn't go very fast. But the members of the Unicorn Rescue Society didn't want to be noticed by whoever was driving it. So they decided to hang back, let it turn a corner, and then follow after it. They tried to look like lost tourists. Which wasn't hard, because they were getting deeper and deeper into the narrow, confusing streets of the old city, *La Habana vieja*.

Finally, the truck stopped. A man and a woman wearing black baseball caps and black T-shirts and black cargo pants got out. They left the engine rumbling and started walking toward the back of the truck. Or toward the members of the Unicorn Rescue Society. It was hard to tell.

So Uchenna quickly pointed up at an apartment house with black wrought iron balconies and asked, loudly, "How old is this one, do you think?"

"Uh, I don't know," said Elliot, in his best impression of a loud American tourist. "Really old, I bet! A thousand years old, maybe?"

"What?" Professor Fauna exclaimed. "Surely, you know better than that, Elliot! While this may be *La Habana vieja*, it is still no older than a hundred and fifty years old. Which is impressive, but one *thousand*? Surely, Elliot—"

"*Stop. Using. His. Name,*" Uchenna hissed through gritted teeth.

"What? Why would I not call Ell—"

Elliot and Uchenna both poked their heads toward the truck with exaggerated movements. Professor Fauna looked. He was not at all subtle. "Oh!" he said. Then he winked at the kids. "Got it. Yes, maybe it *is* a thousand years old! Or a million! I do not know anything! Do you know anything, Elli—uh, Elli*cotty*?" Then he flashed the kids two thumbs up.

Elliot and Uchenna just shook their heads.

Luckily, the truck divers weren't paying attention to anything except what they were doing. They had unloaded a black barrel from the truck and now were carrying it into a small alley.

"*Let's go see what they're up to,*" Uchenna said softly.

"That seems like it's asking for trouble," El-liot replied.

"Oh, the Schmoke Brothers are the ones who have been asking for trouble," Uchenna said slowly. "They've been asking for a *long* while now. And pretty soon, I'm gonna answer."

And with that, Uchenna started for the alley, all by herself.

Elliot gazed after her. "How is she so cool?"

Professor Fauna gazed, too. "I do not know. I have tried to be that cool my whole life."

Elliot cocked an eyebrow at him. "Really?"

Professor Fauna glanced down at Elliot. "Of course not. That was a joke."

"Oh. Right."

"Now," Professor Fauna went on, "a student under my protection is following two henchmen of the most evil men in the world into an alley, in a foreign country she has never visited, completely unsupervised."

"We should go after her."

"*Sí, Elliot. De acuerdo.*"

CHAPTER NINETEEN

Elliot and Professor Fauna hurried after Uchenna. They passed the Schmoke truck, parked in the middle of the street, and caught up to Uchenna at the mouth of an alley so narrow no car could have driven down it.

Elliot crouched down, and Uchenna leaned over him, and the professor leaned over them both, and together they slowly peered around the corner into the alley.

The two black-clad Schmoke employees

dragged a black barrel to the alley's dead end. Then the woman pulled a small crowbar from a loop on her cargo pants and pried off the lid of the barrel. From the opposite end of the alley, the members of the Unicorn Rescue Society couldn't make out what was inside.

The Schmokers tipped the barrel over. Thick pink sludge began to ooze out of the barrel in folds, collecting on top of the sewer grate and then seeping through the bars and into the sewer below.

"That's the sludge that was in the toilet!" Uchenna whispered.

"Why are they dumping out perfectly good sludge?" Professor Fauna whispered back. Elliot and Uchenna both looked up at him. *"What? It seems wasteful!"*

They looked back at the pink ooze pouring into the sewer.

"Unless," Elliot said suddenly, *"they're not wasting it. Maybe it's going* exactly *where they want it to go."*

"Huh?" said Uchenna.

"Into the sewers. Which are connected to the water table. And the bay."

Uchenna's eyes grew wide. *"Like our island model in class! They're poisoning the whole island!"*

"Exactly."

Uchenna stood up. "Okay. They want to keep asking for trouble? Time to answer."

CHAPTER TWENTY

Before Professor Fauna could stop her, Uchenna was walking down the alley, shouting, "Hey! Stop that right now!"

"Um, this is not good," Professor Fauna muttered.

"Yeah. Go get her. And meet me in the street," said Elliot.

"What? Where are *you* going?"

"I've got a hunch." And with that, Elliot was running toward the truck.

"*Children!*" Professor Fauna whispered frantically. Neither heeded him.

"Hey!" Uchenna was shouting. "You two! What is that stuff?"

The Schmokers both let go of the barrel and stood up. The pink sludge continued to glug into the drain. Uchenna stopped walking toward them. Instead, they started walking toward *her*. The man cracked his knuckles. The woman pulled the crowbar from her pantloop again.

Uchenna began wondering if, perhaps, she hadn't made the *wisest* decision.

Then Professor Fauna stepped in front of her.

"*¡Perdón!*" he said.

The Schmokers hesitated.

"*¿Hablan español?*"

"We don't speak Spanish," said the man in an American accent.

"Ah! Of course." Professor Fauna tried his hardest to smile. "Allow me to explain. My student here is *very* enthusiastic about water safety. We are here on a trip from the United States, as, it appears, are you. We are from New Jers—uh, from any state that is *not* New Jersey." He flashed a smile at Uchenna. She stared straight ahead at the Schmokers, who were looking more skeptical by the second. "Anywhat," Professor Fauna went on, "all my friend here can talk about is the bay and the underground aquifer and rainfall and the drought and—"

"Okay," said the woman. She pointed the crowbar at Uchenna. "Just mind your own business, kid."

"Of course," Professor Fauna answered for her. "And I am so sorry. I will upbraid her censoriously."

"We don't speak weirdo, either," said the man. "Now excuse us." The Schmokers pushed past Uchenna and the Professor, leaving the barrel emptying into the sewer behind them, and headed back for their truck.

At the same moment, Elliot was looking in the windows of the truck's cab. There were some papers sitting on the passenger side seat, and a couple of hard hats with the Schmoke *S* on them on the floor. Elliot took a deep breath, glanced at the alley, looked up and down the street to see if anyone else was watching him, and opened the driver side door of the truck.

CHAPTER TWENTY-ONE

The Schmoke employees had just passed Uchenna and the professor, on their way back to the street where they'd left their truck.

"*Hey,*" Uchenna whispered to the professor. "*Where's Elliot?*"

Professor Fauna's eyes widened.

And then, unnaturally loudly, the professor said, "Um, don't you want your barrel?"

The Schmokers turned and looked over their shoulders. "You keep it," said the woman.

"Ah," answered Professor Fauna, "you must not know that littering is illegal in Cuba! I may have to report you to the authorities. The penalties for law-breaking are *very* harsh."

The Schmokers turned and stared at Professor Fauna like he had just done something very, very stupid. "Are you *threatening* us?" the man asked. He cracked his knuckles again, and the woman reached for her crowbar.

"Um, no!" said Professor Fauna. "I would not threaten you! Under the circumstances, that would be, uh . . . unwise!"

"It *sounded* like you were threatening us," said the woman.

"It *did* sound like you were threatening them," Uchenna agreed.

Professor Fauna looked at Uchenna in disbelief.

The Schmokers advanced on them.

"Why would you throw me under the omnibus like that?" Professor Fauna hissed at Uchenna.

The Schmokers came closer.

"Well, I just think you were being rude to these nice, but very littery, tourists," Uchenna replied.

The man cracked his knuckles.

"I do not understand *what* you are trying to do here," Professor Fauna said, exasperated.

Closer.

"Get me beat up?" he went on.

The woman hit her palm with the crowbar.

"Of course not!" Uchenna replied.

Closer.

"I just—"

RRRRUMBLE!

The Schmokers spun around. "Is that our truck?" the man asked.

Uchenna said, "It *sounds* like your truck."

RRRRUMBLE! RRRRUMBLE! RRRRUMBLE! HONNNNNNK!

"Where's it going?" the man demanded.

"I don't know!" cried the woman.

Suddenly, the Schmokers were sprinting out of the alley, away from Uchenna and Professor Fauna.

"What on earth were you doing just now?!" Professor Fauna demanded of Uchenna. "You were putting me in very grave danger!"

"I was improvising! And . . . I hadn't quite figured out how it would end. Sorry. But . . . is Elliot *in* their truck?"

Professor Fauna wrinkled his forehead. Then his eyebrows shot up. "*¡Vaca gigante!* I had not thought of that! After them!"

Uchenna and the professor ran to the end of the alley. When they arrived at the corner, they saw the Schmokers chasing their truck down the narrow street.

Uchenna exclaimed, "Did Elliot *steal their truck*?!?"

"Of course not," said a voice behind them.

Uchenna and Professor Fauna turned around. Elliot was standing there, a clipboard in his hands.

"I would never steal their truck." Then he grinned. "I don't have a driver's license. But I *may* have wedged a hard hat between the accelerator and the bottom of the steering column. Also, I swiped these papers." He waved the clipboard. "Which seem to contain a *lot* of information." Elliot beamed.

But Uchenna said, "Are you telling us that *no one* is driving that truck?"

CRASH!

The truck slammed into the wall of a building.

"Right," said Elliot. The magnitude of his actions was beginning to dawn on him. Plaster fell from the building's wall all over the hood of the truck. A half dozen barrels toppled out of the truck and into the street. "We should probably get out of here."

CHAPTER TWENTY-TWO

Elliot was beginning to come to terms with what he had done.

"I'm a criminal, I'm a criminal, I'm a criminal," he muttered to himself as Professor Fauna knocked on Rosa's door.

"You stole from the *bad guys*," Uchenna reassured him. "They're poisoning Havana's water." And then she added, "For some reason."

"Yes," said Elliot, "but everyone knows that two wrongs don't make a right. They poison. I steal." Elliot threw his head back and raised his hands to the overcast skies. "How does that make *anything* better?!"

"You're being very dramatic."

The door swung open. It was Yoenis. "*¡Mucha-chos!* You have been gone a long time. We were beginning to worry! Come in!"

They entered the shaded walkway beside the garden. Jersey immediately leapt into Elliot's arms. He nuzzled Elliot's chin with his soft, furry head and happily plucked Elliot's sweater with his claws.

"I might as well just throw this sweater away," Elliot grumbled. But he rubbed Jersey's soft back, and that made him feel a little better about his new career as a criminal.

They walked through the garden, and into the bright kitchen, where Rosa had put out a grand spread of pastries. She handed Professor Fauna a mug. "*Café con leche,*" she said.

"Careful," said Yoenis. "My mom makes it very strong and very sweet."

Professor Fauna took a swig. Instantly, he

looked like he'd received an electric shock. He began to suck the *café con leche* from the mug.

Rosa spread her hand out over the pastries. "*Pastelitos. Here,*" she said and picked up a flaky one that oozed with sticky red jam and handed it to Uchenna. "*Guayaba. Buenísimo.*"

"So," said Yoenis, "did you learn anything? About unicorns? Or, more urgently, about our friend the Madre de aguas?"

"Yes, yes, and yes!" Professor Fauna said, thrusting one arm into the air. He tried to take another swig of the *café con leche*, but the mug was already empty. He shook it a few times. He looked at Rosa. "*¿Un poquito más, por favor?*"

Rosa and Yoenis exchanged a glance. But she poured him some more.

"The unicorn story can wait! We have an

urgent matter on our hands! *¡Vengan, vengan, vengan!*" Professor Fauna waved them over to the table. He took out the papers that Elliot had taken from the Schmoke truck.

"Oh!" Elliot moaned. "The fruit of a forbidden tree!"

Uchenna rolled her eyes. "He's just feeling guilty that he took these." And she told Rosa and Yoenis the story.

Rosa tut-tutted. "Don't be too hard on yourself," she told Elliot. "And have a *pastelito de guayaba*." She turned to take one from the plate—and gasped. "Jersey!" Jersey was sitting on the *pastelito* platter, devouring them.

Rosa shooed him off and gave Elliot a slightly mangled *pastelito*. Then she cleaned off the table so they could examine the papers more closely.

CHAPTER TWENTY-THREE

"This is just a random list of addresses and dates," said Yoenis, studying the papers.

At the top of the sheet ran the words, SCHMOKE SURE-TO-CHOKE INSECTICIDE DISTRIBUTION SCHEDULE.

Then, beneath that, were the addresses and dates:

98 CALZADA DE MÁXIMO GÓMEZ, CIENFUEGOS   APRIL I

IO CALLE DE LA TORRE, SANTA CLARA   APRIL I

53 CALLE MARTÍ, CAMAJUANÍ   APRIL 2

1895 CALZADA DE OÑO, SAGUA LA GRANDE   APRIL 4

Flipping to the last pages, Yoenis said, "These here are in Havana. The first ones were all far away."

Every address was marked off except for the last few on the very last page.

Rosa, Yoenis, Uchenna, and Professor Fauna stared at the pages. Jersey was licking *pastelito* crumbs off the floor. Elliot was at the sink, his back to them, washing the sticky *guayaba* off his hands.

"I can't make sense of it," said Yoenis.

Uchenna glanced nervously at Elliot. Then she whispered to Yoenis, *"Did Elliot commit his first crime for nothing?"*

"Technically," whispered Professor Fauna, who

was now shaking from the caffeine and sugar of the *cafés con leche*, "*this was not his first crime. We have committed many crimes together. Breaking and entering. Truancy. Breaking and entering again. Fraud.*" Uchenna could not believe what she was hearing. The professor went on. "*Underage piloting of an unlicensed airplane. Illegal trafficking of an animal across international borders.*" He turned to Rosa, and whispering with fierce urgency for no apparent reason, said, "*May I have another cup of your delicious* café con leche?" Uchenna looked positively frightened of him now.

"Better not, Mito," Rosa said, and patted his quivering hand.

Elliot had come up behind the group and was studying the addresses and dates over Uchenna's shoulder. "These are locations, right?" he said.

"Right," said Yoenis.

"So, the first thing we need is a map."

Uchenna frowned. "You are obsessed with maps."

He smirked at her. "Sometimes obsessions are useful."

So Rosa brought out a map of Cuba.

"You don't happen to have a pink highlighter, do you?" Elliot asked.

"Why pink?" Uchenna asked. And then her eyes lit up "Ohhhh . . ."

"Sorry, *mi'jo*," Rosa said. "I don't have any highlighters."

"Yes, you do," Yoenis said. "I brought you some from Miami!"

"Why? I don't use highlighters."

Yoenis shrugged. "I had some extra room in my bag." He hurried off and came back with a pink highlighter.

"Okay!" said Elliot. "Rosa, if you would read out the addresses, and Yoenis, if you'd find them on the map and mark them in pink, that would be very helpful."

So they began. The first were farms at the distant edges of Cuba, as far from Havana as you could get. But as Rosa kept reading out addresses, the pink crept inland.

"¡Miren!" said Rosa at one point. "That is my brother's farm!"

Yoenis colored it pink.

"What date is next to your brother's farm?" Elliot asked.

"July twenty-first."

"Do you know what happened on July twenty-first at your brother's farm?"

Rosa furrowed her brow. "Not off the top of my head. . . ."

Uchenna looked knowingly at Elliot and then asked, "Is it possible that your brother bought the Schmoke's Sure-to-Choke insecticide around then?"

Rosa's face went pale. "Yes . . . he *was* telling

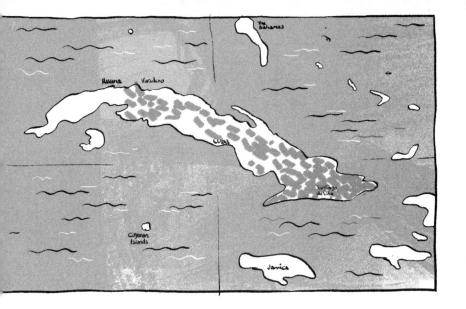

me about this new insecticide that all the farmers were using. . . . He said it worked miracles."

"What's the opposite of a miracle?" Uchenna asked. "Or . . . actually, miracle, but evil?

"A disaster?" Elliot suggested.

"Yes. A disaster. That's what the Sure-to-Choke was."

"Why do you say that?" asked Yoenis.

Elliot answered Yoenis's question with another question: "When did the drought start?"

"This summer, I'd say," Rosa replied. "Or late spring. . . ." And then it was her turn to say, *"Ohh . . ."*

"Keep filling out the map," said Elliot.

CHAPTER TWENTY-FOUR

An hour later, they were nearly finished with the list, and almost all of Cuba looked pink. The only non-pink spot left was Havana. They were working quickly now, Rosa calling out addresses and Yoenis coloring them in. A few minutes later, Havana itself was being encroached upon. Professor Fauna was pacing around the kitchen at sixty miles an hour. Jersey was chasing him.

Suddenly, Rosa gasped.

"What?" Uchenna demanded.

Rosa pointed at an address on the paper. "This is *right behind our house*."

"And what's the date?" Elliot asked.

Rosa said, "About three weeks ago."

"When the Madre de aguas—" Yoenis began.

"—last visited me." His mother completed the thought.

"Just a few more addresses to go," Elliot told them. "Don't stop now."

A few moments later, Rosa read out a number of addresses that ran along the *malecón*. "They're even poisoning the bay!" she spat. "*¡Los diablos!*"

"But why?" Yoenis asked. "The bay doesn't need insecticide!"

"Go on!" Elliot urged them. "Almost there!"

"Almost where?" asked Uchenna.

But Elliot did not answer. He just stared at the map.

They colored in the last few addresses.

"There," said Elliot at last.

Professor Fauna hurried over to see. Jersey's teeth were clamped to his heel.

"The Schmokes have been systematically poisoning Cuba's water supply," said Elliot. "Driving the Madre de aguas out of the hills and valleys, out of the fountains and sewers, and finally even out of the bay."

"Like our island model in class," Uchenna explained. "The Madre de aguas has been fleeing the poison, through the underground water table. But *where* are they driving her *to*?"

"Right there," said Elliot, pointing to the only non-pink spot on the whole map of Cuba. "The

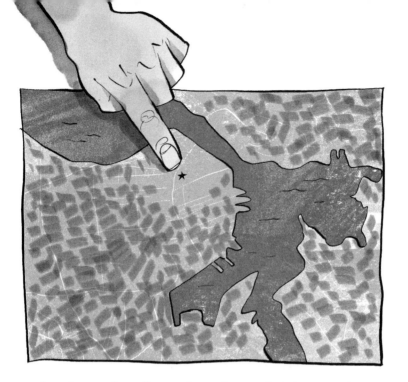

only place they haven't poisoned. That's where they want her to go."

"But what is *THERE?!*" the professor cried, tearing at his hair.

"No more caffeine for him, ever," Rosa muttered.

Yoenis shook his head and looked disgusted with himself. "I should have known." He put his finger on the non-pink spot. "This is the location of the new Schmoke International Hotel."

"But why?" Rosa asked. "Why do they want

my sweet friend at their hotel? What do they plan to *do* with her?"

Yoenis shrugged. Jersey gnawed on the professor's shoelaces.

After a moment, Uchenna said, "Maybe it has something to do with the farmers?"

"The Captains of Agriculture!" Elliot exclaimed.

Rosa looked confused. Yoenis said, "There's a fancy event for the 'Captains of Agriculture' at the Schmoke International Hotel!"

Professor Fauna stood up so forcefully that he knocked his chair over. "*¡Amigos!*" he bellowed. "Let us go on a date with some farmers!"

CHAPTER TWENTY-FIVE

The group stuck close together as they hurried through the streets of Havana toward the new Schmoke Hotel under the heavy gray sky. Elliot led the way. Uchenna followed close behind, the backpack containing Jersey pulled tight against her shoulder blades. Elliot had objected to bringing him ("my sweater just can't take it"), but Uchenna pointed out if they were going to save the Madre de aguas, they should probably bring along the only thing she was afraid of. In case she tried to eat them again.

Behind them came Yoenis and Professor Fauna, who was still recovering from his caffeine infusion and was therefore walking like he'd stepped on an electrified sewer grate.

They came to the plaza with the Schmoke International Hotel. The gleaming marble building with sparkling glass windows towered over old cobblestones, reflecting the clouds that refused to rain overhead.

In front of the hotel, dozens of people stood around in the sunshine, greeting one another, shaking hands, slapping backs, laughing. Some of them were wearing olive-green military uniforms, others were government officials dressed in khakis and nice shirts, while still others wore the faded jeans and *guayaberas* of farmers and ranchers who've just changed after a long day in the fields.

"The Captains of Agriculture," Elliot said, gazing across the plaza at them.

"I guess so," agreed Uchenna.

Jersey chirruped.

"Shh," Elliot told him.

Uchenna studied the hotel and considered their options. They could try to blend into the crowd entering the hotel—but there was probably a guest list. Besides, who would believe that two kids were Captains of Agriculture?

Yoenis tapped Uchenna on the shoulder and indicated that they should follow him.

Around the side of the hotel there was a service

entrance tucked away behind a row of royal palms. Servers in black and white uniforms rolled carts laden with silver platters up a ramp and into the hotel. The members of the Unicorn Rescue Society loitered casually, watching them work.

Uchenna spoke softly to Elliot, "You don't happen to have four black serving uniforms with you, do you?"

"Nope."

"I do," said Yoenis. They all looked at him like he was joking. "I brought them from the States. They're in my suitcase at my mom's."

Elliot said, "I swear you are Mary Poppins." He pointed. "That cart is pretty big." Near the base of the ramp, a server was carefully arranging a frilly white cloth over a cart.

"And we're pretty small. . . ." Uchenna added. "If Yoenis or Professor Fauna could create a distraction . . ."

"Professor Fauna would be delighted to create a distraction!!!" Professor Fauna announced.

"It is his specialty!!!" He strode forward with an enormous smile.

"*Buenas,*" he said to the server who had been arranging the cart. "*¡¡¡¿¿¿Tremendo evento esta tarde, no???!!!*"

The server wiped his brow on his shirtsleeve. "*Sí, señor.*"

"*¡Me encantaría si me invitaran!*"

The server looked confused.

"What's he saying?"

Yoenis turned away so the server wouldn't see him stifling a laugh. "He says he wants to be invited to the party."

"*¿Me puedes conseguir una invitación? ¡Y ropa elegante, claro! No conozco a los capitanes de la agricultura, pero si los conociera seríamos buenos amigos!*"

"He says he doesn't know the Captains of Agriculture yet, but he's sure they'd be great friends."

Elliot muffled a guffaw in his sleeve. Uchenna said, "C'mon."

Uchenna and Elliot darted forward and

hurried into the hollow bottom of the serving cart. Elliot crouched, making himself as small as possible, while Uchenna arranged the white frilly cloth to hide them.

Only the slightest bit of gray light filtered through the cloth, and it was dark and cramped in the cart. Elliot was sweating. Not a moment too soon, they heard Fauna say, *"¡Una pena! ¡Un día de estos tienen que pasar por mi casa! ¡Adiós! ¡Nos vemos pronto!"* and the cart began to move. They

could see the server's shoes as he pushed them up the ramp, grunting from the weight and mumbling to himself about *"El hombre loco."* With one more big push, the cart rolled swiftly through the side door.

Through the white cloth Uchenna and Elliot saw a thousand flickers of golden light. They had made it into the grand, chandelier-filled lobby of the Schmoke International Hotel.

CHAPTER TWENTY-SIX

Elliot and Uchenna held still and listened hard. The banquet hadn't started yet. They heard silverware clinking onto plates and chairs being unloaded from handcarts. Elliot and Uchenna waited.

Finally, the servers left, and Uchenna and Elliot heard only a steady rushing sound, like a fan running on high. After a few quiet moments, Uchenna poked her head out from under the cloth.

The lobby was even more grand than she had imagined. The ceilings were so tall it was like being in a cathedral. A wide black marble staircase led up to the second floor. And the rushing sound they had heard wasn't a fan at all: It was the fountain made of gold. Uchenna squinted.

It can't be.

Elliot poked his head out next to hers. *"The fountain is shaped like the Madre de aguas?!"*

From within the lobby, the shape of the fountain was unmistakable. It was clearly the Madre

de aguas. Water shot out of horns rendered in gold and cascaded into the pool below.

Near the fountain was a tower of nine black barrels of Schmoke's Sure-to-Choke insecticide.

Uchenna said, "Come on, let's make a run for one of the tables."

No sooner had they climbed out of the cart than they heard footsteps, tip-tapping down the marble staircase into the lobby.

"Hurry!" Uchenna urged Elliot, who dove under the nearest table.

At which point, Elliot almost screamed.

Two people were *already* hiding under the table.

Luckily, the two people were Yoenis and Professor Fauna.

"How did you get here?" Uchenna hissed at them.

Yoenis said, *"The professor told one of the guards outside that he was the Captain of the Captains of Agriculture. The dude was so confused he just let us in."*

Just then, a growl emanated from Jersey's backpack.

"Shh!" whispered Elliot. *"Someone's coming!"*

All they could see from under the table was feet walking by. Two pairs of feet, wearing black leather shoes with tassels. The leather was so shiny it could have been a mirror.

"Well, Milton," said a voice, "our plan has worked to perfection."

Uchenna and Elliot locked eyes.

"Of course it did, Edmund. It was *our* plan."

The Schmoke Brothers were in Havana.

Right next to them.

CHAPTER TWENTY-SEVEN

Edmund Schmoke was saying to his brother Milton, "The farmers really ate up that Sure-To-Choke insecticide."

"Everyone did," said Milton. "It's all over their fruits and vegetables!"

They both laughed.

"Who is that?" Yoenis asked in a whisper that was barely a breath.

"The Schmoke Brothers," Elliot replied.

"The tanker truck is coming in an hour," Edmund announced. "And make sure you *do not mention* the location of our fishy friend while in the hotel. The servers and help are *not* to be trusted. By tomorrow she'll be in Florida, and our Everglades bottling operation will be underway!"

Milton chuckled. "Those farmers will be *begging* us for our bottled water. By next week these poor Cubans will be our best customers."

"*My* favorite part is, the Cubans won't know it's *their own* water we're selling to them!"

"Ha-HA-ha!"

"Ha-ha-HA!"

"Now," Milton went on, returning to a brisk tone. "I'm handling this meeting. We have to seal the deal; make sure the people know that *we* are their water source."

"Oh, the deal shall be sealed. As tightly as a bottle of Schmokey Mountain Natural Spring Water."

"Which is bottled nowhere near the Smoky Mountains."

"Hence 'Schmokey.' Legally airtight."

"*Water*tight!"

"Ha-HA-ha-ha!"

"Ha-ha-HA-ha!"

"*These guys have the weirdest sense of humor,*" Uchenna whispered.

Elliot shushed her.

"Ahh . . ." Edmund Schmoke sighed as their laughter subsided. "It is delightful being smarter than everyone else."

"Isn't it?" his brother agreed. It sounded like he was removing a handkerchief from his pocket and wiping tears of mirth from his eyes.

A bell chimed, and Uchenna and Elliot could hear the sound of servers reentering the lobby. The Schmokes ended their conversation and sauntered off.

"*We've got to stop all of this,*" Uchenna whispered. "*Job number one is to save the Madre de agaus from those oily pieces of garbage. But we also can't let these folks get duped by the Schmokes!"*

"You two find the Madre de aguas," Yoenis told them. He gestured at the professor. "Twitchy here and I will figure out a way to disrupt this meeting. Right, Twitchy?"

Professor Fauna's right eyebrow was going up and down like a sideways metronome.

"Okay," said Elliot. "Let's go."

CHAPTER TWENTY-EIGHT

U chenna and Elliot moved fast, crawling from table to table and ultimately into the hallway that led to the kitchen. There, they leaned against the wall to catch their breath.

Uchenna, between inhales and exhales, asked Elliot, "Where could you even keep the Madre de aguas in a hotel? She's enormous! Or at least, she can be when she wants to be."

"And she *makes water*," Elliot went on. "I mean, look at this carpeting." He shifted his weight over the deep plush carpet in the hallway. "If I spilled even a teaspoon of water on a carpet like this, Bubbe would murder me."

Uchenna punched Elliot in the arm.

"Ow!"

"Elliot, you're a genius." Uchenna peeled herself off the wall and marched down the hallway to the elevator, where a hotel directory hung next to a stairwell. "There's only one place you could keep that much water in a hotel."

Elliot came up next to Uchenna as she ran her fingers down the list of different locations.

Roof Deck—Roof
Spa—Sky Lobby
Anti-Balding Center—Sky Lobby
Money Counting Chamber—13th Floor
Ballrooms—Mezzanine Level
Diamond Rooms—Upper Mezzanine Level
Lobby—Ground Floor
Fancy Private Lobby for the Embarrassingly
    Wealthy—Ground Floor, Other Side

Elliot's finger stopped.

Pool –Basement

"There," said Elliot.

Uchenna nodded. She pointed at the bright glow of the emergency exit sign, right above the stairwell beside them. They pushed open the door and broke into a run down the stairs, plunging deeper and deeper into the bowels of the Schmoke Hotel, Jersey squeaking every time his backpack bounced against Uchenna's back.

The farther down they went, the more the smell of chlorine filled their nostrils. It smelled

way worse than a normal hotel swimming pool. It was so strong that Elliot felt his eyes burning, and Uchenna thought she might gag.

They reached the basement and pushed through enormous glass doors that opened onto a bigger-than-Olympic-sized swimming pool below an arched brick ceiling.

And in that bigger-than-Olympic-sized swimming pool was a huge scaly creature with ornate horns, midnight-blue eyes, and a body like the biggest snake that's ever lived.

Except this time, the Madre de aguas didn't rise to meet them. She didn't even raise her head. She wasn't moving at all.

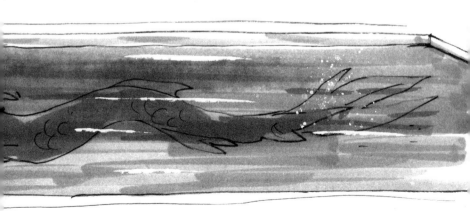

CHAPTER TWENTY-NINE

"Is she . . ." Uchenna couldn't even finish her sentence. The Madre de aguas floated, lifeless, in the Schmoke Hotel swimming pool.

"No," Elliot said quietly. "They wouldn't do that. They need her for their bottling business, remember?"

They watched her a few minutes longer, and to Uchenna's relief, her body swelled and contracted . . . just slightly. She was breathing. Though barely.

"It must be all the chlorine,"

Elliot went on. "We know she doesn't react well to—"

"*Welcome!*" said a booming voice.

Elliot and Uchenna grabbed each other and looked around wildly. The voice echoed; it seemed to be coming from everywhere at once.

"*Thank you so much for joining us!*"

Elliot whispered, "Who's saying that?"

Then Uchenna pointed at a vent in the ceiling. Elliot exhaled.

It was the meeting, getting underway.

"*Why yes,*" Milton Schmoke was saying, "*there does seem to be a drought in Cuba. We have no idea why!*"

"*But,*" Edmund continued, "*we would be more than happy to provide water to the tourism industry and to the farmers of Cuba!*"

"*For a very modest fee,*" said Milton.

Uchenna and Elliot locked eyes. There was no time to lose.

Back upstairs in the banquet hall, Yoenis and Fauna were gathering their courage. They were huddled together under the very center of the table, trying to avoid letting any of the guests' knees or shoes touch them.

"You have all been such excellent customers of our Sure-to-Choke insecticide!" Milton Schmoke was saying. He and his brother were framed by the tower of nine black barrels.

"And it works, does it not?" Edmund added. "Have you ever seen an insecticide that works so well?"

One of the farmers said loudly, "It is hard to tell if it works, or if the *sequía* has gotten so bad that all the insects just *died*."

"Indeed, indeed!

So, one way or another, it works!" Edmund said, smiling. There were some confused murmurs from the guests.

"Moving right along!" Milton said quickly. "We solved your bug problem. Now we will solve your drought problem! In front of you, you will find contracts for the importation of Schmokey Mountain Natural Spring Water! As much as you need! Just turn to the last page of the contract before you—please ignore all that fine print, it's meaningless legal jargon—pick up the Schmoke International Hotel pen that is sitting next to the contracts—complimentary! You're welcome!— and sign on the dotted line!"

"Trust us! You'll be sorry!" added Edmund. His brother shot him a look. "If you don't sign, I mean!" Edmund tried to laugh pleasantly.

There was more uncertain muttering from the assembled Captains of Agriculture.

Yoenis touched Professor Fauna's shoulder.

"*¿Ahora?*" he murmured.

"*¡AHORA!*" Professor Fauna shouted, standing straight up and toppling the table over, with much crashing of glass and silverware.

"*¡Mentirosos!*" Professor Fauna cried, pointing at the Schmoke brothers. Then he turned to the farmers. "*Primero, me presento. ¡Yo voy a ser su mejor amigo . . . en cuanto vengan a mi casa!*"

The guests stared. The servers stopped. Milton and Edmund Schmoke were so startled that they forgot the rest of their speech. "What did he say?" Edmund stammered.

"He just invited us all to his house," a farmer translated.

CHAPTER THIRTY

Yoenis put his hand on Professor Fauna's shoulder. "Professor, I'll handle this."

Yoenis turned to the crowd and said, *"Perdonen por la interrupción, pero, ¡estos señores sí están mintiendo! Su insecticida es peligroso. Solo lo vendieron para envenenar el agua y traer a la Madre de aguas al hotel, para enjaularla y usarla para su negocio de agua embotellada!"*

A man in a black suit scurried up to Edmund and Milton Schmoke and whispered in their ears.

Their translator, Yoenis thought, and went on in more rapid and fluent Spanish.

Yoenis explained the Schmoke Brothers' scheme to capture the Madre de aguas and bottle the water she produced and sell it back to Cuba. The guests began to murmur to one another. Comprehension, and then anger, dawned on their faces.

Once the translator had caught them up, Edmund Schmoke exclaimed, "The Madre de aguas? What kind of nonsense is that? Milton and I are far too intelligent to believe such silly legends! We've never even *heard* of the Madre de aguas."

The Captains of Agriculture turned to see how Yoenis would respond to this denial.

Yoenis said, "If you've never heard of the Madre de aguas . . . why would you make it *the centerpiece of your fountain?!*" He pointed at the gaudy golden fountain, spewing water merrily from its horns.

The heads of every Captain of Agriculture swiveled toward the fountain. And a roar erupted from them all.

The Schmokes began to stammer:

"Uh . . . we . . . we didn't know that was the Madre de aguas!"

"Uh . . . right!"

"Some peasant artisan made it for us! For cheap!"

"Exactly! No . . . expensive! We only like expensive things."

"Of course! Yes! We just thought it was . . . a . . . a . . . weird, overgrown tadpole!"

A farmer stood up so fast his chair fell over. "Tadpole? *¿En serio?*" he demanded. "The Madre de aguas has visited my well and kept my farm going for years and years! At least, she did, until recently."

"She used to visit my creek, too!" shouted a bearded farmer from the back. "I had tons of fresh water . . . before you two came along with your pink poison!"

Another farmer stood. "We can all thank Oshún for all the sweet waters in Cuba. And *these* two slimy *serpientes*," she snapped at the Schmokes, "have disrespected her!"

"Now, now, *mi gente*," said a farmer with a wide-brimmed hat, also standing up. "Every good Catholic knows that we get fresh water from María, Mother of God. May she keep us safe from evildoers—like the Schmokes!"

"Don't be silly!" said a communist official, wearing a suit and a green armband with a red star. "Those are old-fashioned beliefs! That is a statue of a snake, the *majá*! And all the animals of Cuba deserve to be protected!" He cleared his throat. "To honor the animals of Cuba, I will recite our national anthem!" And he began to sing:

"*Al combate, corred, bayameses . . .*"

The farmer with the wide-brimmed hat

announced, "Then I'll pray! *Oh, santísima Virgen de la Caridad, Madre mía . . ."*

"Oshún, daughter of the river!" intoned another farmer.

Yoenis had jumped up on a table, taken by the spirit of the moment. "I invoke the father of our liberty and the champion of the Cuban people, José Martí!" And he began reciting a poem.

"Cultivo una rosa blanca . . .
En julio como en enero,
Para el amigo sincero
Que me da su mano franca.
Y para el cruel que me arranca
El corazón con que vivo,
Cardo ni oruga cultivo:
Cultivo la rosa blanca."

And then he said it in English, for the benefit of the Schmokes:

"I grow a white rose

In July and in January;

I give it to my true friend,

Who gives me his hand.

And for the bully whose insults

Break my heart,

I give him neither weeds nor worms:

For him, too, I have a white rose."

The walls of the ornate hotel lobby filled with the sounds of people singing, praying, and reciting poetry. They were all celebrating the Madre

de aguas, or Oshún, or Mary—or, simply, Cuba—
with their words. Milton and Edmund Schmoke
stared. The voices of hundreds—farmers, government workers, and servers—were twining around
one another's, like the roots of a ceiba tree, twisting and twining into one trunk.

"What on earth is happening?" Milton muttered.

"I am not sure, brother," Edmund replied.

Milton Schmoke shouted at the top of his
lungs. "We are offering you a once-in-a-lifetime
business opportunity! Business! Money! ¡*Dinero!*
Don't you simpletons *hear* me?!"

Edmund was disgusted. "Don't try to reason
with them. They're hopeless. Security! Security!"
He pointed at Yoenis and Professor Fauna. "Ap-
prehend the trespassers!"

"Yeah!" shouted Milton. "Get 'em!"

CHAPTER THIRTY-ONE

Down by the pool, Elliot and Uchenna were desperately trying to rouse the Madre de aguas.

"If we can't get her moving, we can't get her out of here," Elliot was saying. "Do you have the water bottle?"

Uchenna unzipped the backpack and took out a Miami Marlins water bottle that Yoenis had brought for his mom. When she did, Jersey tried to spring free. "Not yet, little guy," Uchenna said. "We know you're ready for action, but we need a plan." Jersey growled at her in frustration. Uchenna handed Elliot the water bottle.

"So we have this water bottle," said Elliot. "But how are we gonna convince her to get into it?"

Uchenna shrugged.

"And what if we *do* get her in, and then she explodes out of it and kills us?"

Uchenna shrugged again.

Elliot hung his head. "This plan is pathetic."

Uchenna, gently, said, "It was *your* plan."

"That's why I said it was pathetic. I wouldn't have said that about a plan *you* came up with."

Uchenna smiled. "You're sweet."

Suddenly, Jersey's bag erupted with a very frightening growl.

Uchenna said, "Uh . . . we've never heard him make that sound before."

Elliot agreed. "He sounds *angry*. At us."

Jersey growled again.

"I'm letting him out," said Uchenna.

Elliot shrugged feebly.

Uchenna unzipped the bag. Jersey burst out of it.

He began sprinting around the exterior of the pool, growling and yapping at the Madre de aguas.

And then, the giant sea serpent stirred.

"Look! She's moving!" Uchenna cried.

The Madre de aguas blinked her eyes heavily.

Jersey yipped at her some more.

Slowly, very slowly, she raised her giant head.

He yapped. She began to shrink, and as she did, she swam away from him.

"It's working!"

Jersey began running around the pool again. Uchenna and Elliot started to run, too—keeping themselves on the opposite side of the pool from Jersey. Sure enough, the Madre de aguas started right for them, to get as far away from the tiny blue Jersey Devil as possible. His yips and yaps were rousing her from her stupor. As she got smaller and more frightened, she began to move more and more swiftly, and the water from the pool began to overflow onto the floor tiles.

"Get the water bottle ready!" Elliot cried. But he needn't have said anything. Uchenna was ready.

Jersey yipped and yapped and growled. The Madre de aguas swam closer to them, and closer, and—

A strange sound was coming through the vent that led to the lobby. There was shouting, and crashing. And then . . . *singing?* What was going *on* up there? It sounded like singing and chanting, all mixed together.

The Madre de aguas froze.

"Oh, come *on*," Uchenna urged her, holding the water bottle as far out over the pool as she could. "Come just a little closer . . . just a *little* closer . . ."

The chanting grew louder as more voices joined in, each with a different song or prayer. But each voice seemed to weave smoothly into the greater whole. Like the music they'd heard in the plaza.

"She *likes* the chanting," Elliot marveled.

The words began to weave together, each prayer and song so different, becoming one:

"Al combate . . ."

"For my friend . . ."

"Cuba . . ."

"Of the sweet waters . . ."

"Oh, santísima . . ."

"*Amigo sincero . . .*"

"*Madre mía . . .*"

"*Cuba . . .*"

Suddenly, the Madre de aguas started swimming away from Uchenna. Toward the bottom of the pool.

"No!" Uchenna groaned. And then, "Wait, where is she going?"

"Looks like . . . ," said Elliot, ". . . to the drain?"

Sure enough, the Madre de aguas swam right for the drain at the deepest point of the pool. She started wriggling at the white plastic mesh of the drain, getting so tiny she was almost invisible. And then, she disappeared.

"Wow. Our plan *literally* went down the drain," Elliot said. But then he said, "Wait! I have a theory!" And he plunged his head under the water.

"Elliot!"

Elliot reemerged, dripping with heavily chlorinated pool water. "I was right!" he announced.

"You can hear the chant-ing, amplified by the water! It must be coming through the water pipes, too! I think she's following the singing!"

"Yeah, maybe," said Uchenna. "But look . . ."

Elliot looked at where Uchenna was pointing.

His face lost all color.

She was pointing at his sweater.

It was changing colors very rapidly.

"Must be from all the chlorine. I don't even know what that new color is *called*," Uchenna marveled. "Toxic pink?"

Elliot hung his head in despair.

CHAPTER THIRTY-TWO

A dozen men and women in black shirts and black baseball hats and black cargo pants had appeared in the lobby. The Captains of Agriculture were so busy singing and praying and reciting their poems that they didn't notice. But Yoenis and Professor Fauna did.

"Not *them* again," Professor Fauna muttered.

"You know these guys?" Yoenis wondered.

"Old friends."

The Schmoke security guards created a circle

around Yoenis, up on the table, and the professor, who stood beside it.

"Maybe *they* want to have a slumber part—"

BOOM!

Professor Fauna and Yoenis spun around just in time to see the golden statue of the Madre de aguas *explode.*

Shards of gold and steel shot in every direction, hitting the ceiling and the chandelier, causing glass and plaster to mix with the gold and steel to rain down on everyone. Chlorinated pool water surged out of the fountain and flooded the floor.

"*¡Es ella!*" someone cried. "It's really her!"

As the haze of plaster, glass, and gold cleared, the crowd saw a mighty sea serpent uncoiling, shaking off the bits of statue she'd broken through, growing and rising and growing, sucking up all the water that coursed through the Schmoke Hotel's water system—until she touched the ceiling.

Everyone gaped.

"That's even bigger than she was in the bay. . . ." Professor Fauna murmured.

"That's bigger than I ever imagined. . . ." Yoenis replied.

The Madre de aguas looked around the banquet hall as if she were searching for something. Finally, her eyes rested on the tall glass windows and the glimmer of the sea just visible in the distance.

Her body rippled and vibrated with strength, and she tore away from the fountain and plowed through the tables, reducing them to wood chips and tatters of white fabric. She smashed through the display of Sure-to-Choke insecticide, toppling the barrels over and spilling the pink sludge on the plush carpeting. Then she burst through the huge windows and, carried on a river of water that she secreted from her body, she escaped down one of the small alleys of Old Havana, toward the *malecón* and the sparkling bay.

The room exploded with cheers. Farmers and

bureaucrats and servers alike stamped their feet and whistled.

At just that moment, Elliot and Uchenna burst through the doors from the service stairs. "What happened?" Elliot asked. Uchenna shook her head. Jersey flew up beside them.

And then they noticed two figures, one short and one tall, sitting by the overturned black barrels, covered in pink sludge. It covered their ten-thousand dollar suits. It covered their monogrammed shirts. It even covered their matching comb-overs.

"Help us!" the Schmokes cried. "This stuff is toxic!"

"What did you say?" Professor Fauna asked. He was pushing his way past the security guards, toward the Schmokes.

Yoenis hushed the crowd.

"This stuff is pure poison!" Edmund Schmoke was wailing. "Please, please get it off!"

Even their security team didn't want to touch

them. They just stood there, grimacing at the horrific pink mess.

"You want a napkin?" Professor Fauna asked, gabbing two from a nearby table and dangling one over each of the Schmoke's heads.

"Yes!"

"Then tell these good people of your plans."

"We were going to steal her!" Milton cried. "And sell you the water she produced for us!"

"We admit it!" Edmund shouted. "Just get

this stuff off of us! It smells like the runoff from our oil refineries!"

"It *is* the runoff from our oil refineries!" Milton moaned. "Just please, help us!"

Professor Fauna dropped the napkins and the Schmokes grabbed them, madly rubbing the pink sludge from their faces.

In the distance, there was giant splash. The Madre de aguas had made it back into the bay.

CHAPTER THIRTY-THREE

Elliot and Uchenna hugged Yoenis a thousand times, and then they hugged Rosa a thousand times, and then they hugged Yoenis again.

They were all standing at the edge of the *malecón*, beside where Maceo's garbage barge was docked. And sitting on the broad sidewalk, obstructing all pedestrian traffic, was the *Phoenix*. It gleamed. Maceo was shining the nose of the plane.

"I don't think the *Phoenix* looked this nice when she was new," Professor Fauna marveled.

"That plane was *new* once?" Rosa asked. They all laughed.

"Well," said Elliot. "Shall we head home?"

"Indeed, my friends," the professor agreed. "I think it is—"

BOOM!

Everyone fell silent.

"What was that?" Uchenna asked.

Elliot looked up.

BOOM!

Elliot closed his eyes. "Thunder," he said.

And at that moment, the clouds opened and rain began to pour out of the sky.

"The *sequía* is over! It's over!" Rosa cried. Yoenis grabbed her, and they began to dance in the heavy rain. Jersey flapped around them, flying curlicues in time to their steps. "Do you doubt now?" Rosa called to Professor Fauna. "The Schmokes are leaving, the Madre de aguas is free, and look! She is happy again, and the rain falls!"

Uchenna glanced at Elliot. Elliot said, "This

proves nothing. There's been a twenty-five per-cent chance all day."

Uchenna said, "There's been a twenty-five percent chance for *months*. This seems like a *coincidence* to you?"

Elliot opened his mouth, but then he closed it again. He smiled, and shrugged.

Rosa crowed as she danced, "Like two roots of the ceiba! You two don't have to agree to be one tree! Now," she said, "before you get in that plane, you better dance with us! *¡Vengan! ¡Bailen!*"

Professor Fauna leaned into the *Phoenix* and

turned on the radio as loud as it could go. A hypnotic, irresistible song arose from the tinny speakers: a guitar, a conga drum, and a *güiro* played together, twining and twisting around one another. And the members of the Unicorn Rescue Society joined Yoenis, Rosa, and Jersey, as they danced on the *malecón* in the sweet, sweet rain.

A HISTORY OF

The Secret Order of the Unicorn

(Being the History of the Secret Organization, Founded in the Year 789, That Exists to Protect Unicorns from All Humans Who Might Hurt Them)

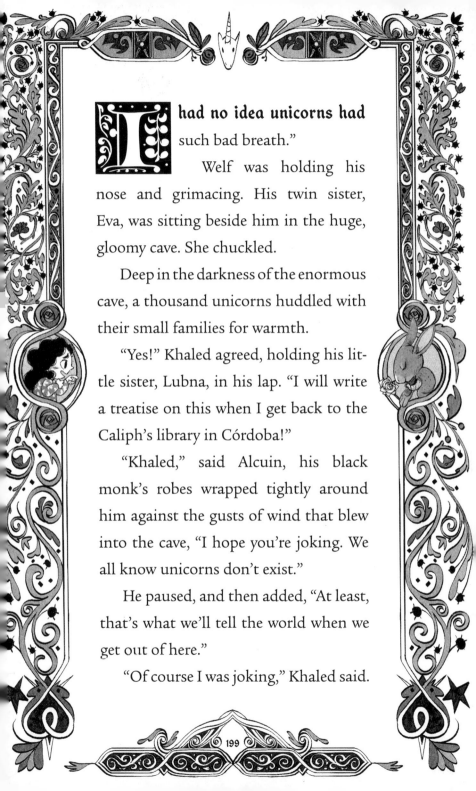

I had no idea unicorns had such bad breath."

Welf was holding his nose and grimacing. His twin sister, Eva, was sitting beside him in the huge, gloomy cave. She chuckled.

Deep in the darkness of the enormous cave, a thousand unicorns huddled with their small families for warmth.

"Yes!" Khaled agreed, holding his little sister, Lubna, in his lap. "I will write a treatise on this when I get back to the Caliph's library in Córdoba!"

"Khaled," said Alcuin, his black monk's robes wrapped tightly around him against the gusts of wind that blew into the cave, "I hope you're joking. We all know unicorns don't exist."

He paused, and then added, "At least, that's what we'll tell the world when we get out of here."

"Of course I was joking," Khaled said.

"You thought I'd write a treatise about unicorns' bad breath?"

"Ah," said Alcuin. "Of course. Sorry. I'm pretty hungry."

"So are we all," Eva said, gazing around at the small, sad group, huddled around a dead fire. "But on the bright side, I'm pretty sure the secret of the unicorns is safe. Because I'm pretty sure we're *all* going to starve to death . . . trapped in a remote cave . . . surrounded by the most impassable and treacherous mountains in the world."

The young nun, Gisela, was stroking her gray bunny. Just then, he jumped from her lap and hopped to the opening of the cave and stared out at the deep drifts of snow that coated the slopes of the towering, craggy mountains.

"What do you think, Bunny?" Eva called. "Are we going to be stranded here forever?"

It *really* looked like the bunny nodded.

Lubna pushed herself off of Khaled's knee and shouted, "Bunny play! Bunny play!"

Alcuin cursed under his breath. "Who would have expected a snowstorm in *June*? Two days into our mountain journey, all sunshine and wildflowers, and then *boom*. Instant winter. Trapping us in this freezing, barren cave."

"With a thousand starving unicorns," Eva added.

"And their breath," said Welf.

"Pretty!" Lubna was running back toward them. "Pretty!" She was pointing at the snow outside.

Khaled sighed. "Yes, Lubna. The snow is pretty."

But Lubna shouted, "No!" And started to cry.

"I'm with you, kid," Welf muttered.

Just then, they heard the sounds of scuffling hooves and angry whinnying from deeper in the cave.

The humans all looked at one another.

The sounds got worse.

Angrier.

"Should we see what's going on?" Eva asked nervously.

"You mean, should we wander into the darkest part of this cave, with no lantern or fire, and try to break up a fight amongst a thousand angry, starving unicorns?" Welf asked. "Sure. That sounds fun."

Eva stood up. "I'm going."

Khaled rose, too. "So am I."

Lubna cried louder: "Pretty! Pretty! Oony-corn yum yum!"

Khaled looked pleadingly at Sister Gisela. Without a word, she nodded, stood up, and took Lubna's little hand. Lubna stopped crying and led Gisela to the front of the cave, where the gray bunny was sniffing at the snow.

Lubna was still muttering, "Oony-corn yum yum pretty. Oony-corn yum yum pretty."

The cave was not *entirely* dark. There were a thousand dimly glowing horns, on the tops of a thousand unicorn heads. It was like walking through a forest at night with no stars and no moon, but where the branches of the trees glowed.

Khaled and Eva walked side by side, their shoulders touching. They made their way around families of unicorns, lying on the cold, wet stone, or standing in tight groups. Their horns were a hundred different hues.

The unicorns were restless, agitated. Because they were hungry, but also because of the sounds of fighting that were coming from deeper within the cave. And the sounds were getting worse.

The scrape of horn on stone.

The cry of a unicorn.

Eva started to run, and Khaled was close behind her. He stumbled over a unicorn's outstretched leg, and fell,

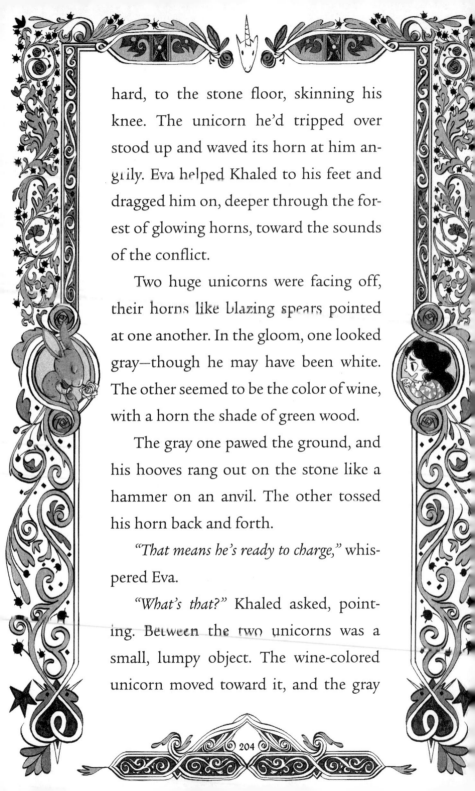

hard, to the stone floor, skinning his knee. The unicorn he'd tripped over stood up and waved its horn at him angrily. Eva helped Khaled to his feet and dragged him on, deeper through the forest of glowing horns, toward the sounds of the conflict.

Two huge unicorns were facing off, their horns like blazing spears pointed at one another. In the gloom, one looked gray—though he may have been white. The other seemed to be the color of wine, with a horn the shade of green wood.

The gray one pawed the ground, and his hooves rang out on the stone like a hammer on an anvil. The other tossed his horn back and forth.

"That means he's ready to charge," whispered Eva.

"What's that?" Khaled asked, pointing. Between the two unicorns was a small, lumpy object. The wine-colored unicorn moved toward it, and the gray

one jabbed the air with his horn to make him fall back.

"It looks like . . . food," said Eva. "The last of the hay we passed around yesterday morning."

"They're going to kill each other over a lump of stale hay?"

"They're starving."

Just then, Eva and Khaled heard the sound of two small feet, moving very quickly.

Before they could react, Lubna ran out in front of them, directly toward the two angry unicorns. "Pretty oony-corn yum yum! Pretty oony-corn yum yum!"

"Lubna, stop!" Khaled cried.

Gisela came running up beside them, shouting, "Lubna, come back!"

But it was too late.

The gray unicorn reared up, his forehooves kicking the air. The wine-colored unicorn whinnied with rage.

"*LUBNA!*" Khaled shrieked.

The gray unicorn came crashing down.

Eva screamed. Khaled screamed. Gisela screamed.

Lubna did not scream.

Because she was encircled by four young unicorns.

They had dashed out of the darkness to protect the little girl.

Lubna put her tiny hand on the flank of one of the young unicorns.

"Oony-corn pretty yum yum!" she said.

And then she held up a flower.

"Where did she get *that*?" Khaled murmured.

"Oony-corn! Oony-corn!" said Lubna. The young unicorn she was touching turned its head to her, lowered its long face, and sniffed.

"Yum yum!" said Lubna.

The unicorn nibbled at the flower. Then the unicorn ate it whole, and sucked up the stem with its big soft lips.

Lubna clapped. "Pretty! Pretty!" she cried. "Oony-corn yum yum!" And she went running toward the mouth of the cave, and the bright, deep snow.

The young unicorns followed her.

After a moment, the other unicorns did, too.

Eva and Khaled and Gisela stared.

At the mouth of the cave, the bunny hopped around on the packed snow, snuffling with his soft gray nose. Every few hops, he would stop, and then start digging with his forepaws, until a tiny white blossom would appear. He would nibble at the blossom, and then suck up the stem, just as the young unicorn had done.

When Lubna arrived, she pointed at what the bunny was doing and said, "Pretty yum yum!" And when the young unicorns came even with her, she added, "Oony-corn pretty yum yum!"

The young unicorns moved out into

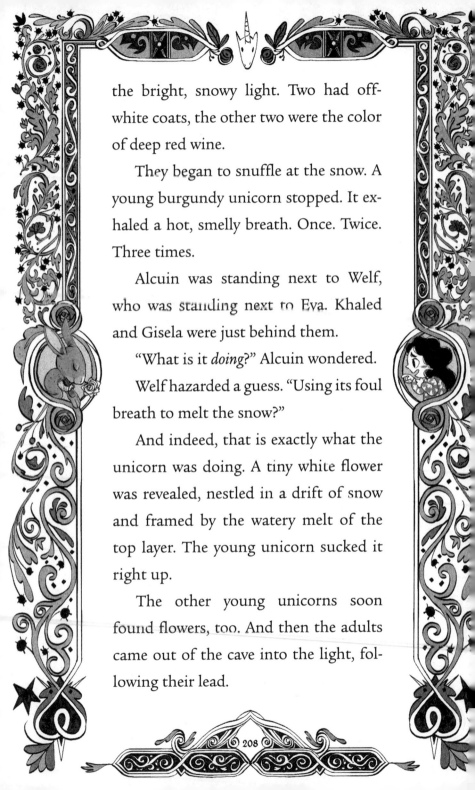

the bright, snowy light. Two had off-white coats, the other two were the color of deep red wine.

They began to snuffle at the snow. A young burgundy unicorn stopped. It exhaled a hot, smelly breath. Once. Twice. Three times.

Alcuin was standing next to Welf, who was standing next to Eva. Khaled and Gisela were just behind them.

"What is it *doing*?" Alcuin wondered.

Welf hazarded a guess. "Using its foul breath to melt the snow?"

And indeed, that is exactly what the unicorn was doing. A tiny white flower was revealed, nestled in a drift of snow and framed by the watery melt of the top layer. The young unicorn sucked it right up.

The other young unicorns soon found flowers, too. And then the adults came out of the cave into the light, following their lead.

"Oony-corn pretty yum yum!" Lubna cheered, clapping her little hands gleefully.

The members of the Secret Order of the Unicorn stared as a thousand unicorns emerged from the cave and into the sunny, snow-covered mountains, and began to melt the snow, until they were standing in a huge meadow, covered in patches of snow and white wildflowers. Which they ate to their hearts' content.

"This," said Welf, "is the weirdest thing I have ever seen."

"Weird and beautiful," Alcuin replied. "Weird and beautiful."

Gisela had picked up her bunny and was stroking its head. Very quietly, she said, "I think we just might make it after all."

And do you know what?

She was right.

TO BE CONCLUDED . . .

ACKNOWLEDGMENTS

WE WOULD LIKE TO THANK Professor Raquel Otheguy, who introduced Emma and Adam to one another many years ago, and who has provided incomparable love and support for both of us, and to our spouses and families. Raquel also provided a beautiful description of the Cuban National Archives and the people there. (We used some of her account verbatim!)

We are deeply grateful to Olugbemisola Rhuday-Perkovich, who read this book with a focus on Yoruba culture. Olugbemisola was a member of the Unicorn Rescue Society long before a single book in this series was published; we think of her as Uchenna's cool aunt who makes sure her niece is up to date on all the latest music.

David Bowles, another longtime member of the Unicorn Rescue Society, workshopped the end of this novel with Adam one morning, sitting on a bench in Brooklyn. The intertwining of the voices from different cultures—calling forth the Madre de aguas—was his brilliant suggestion.

Professor Anasa Hicks, Emma's longtime friend and scholar of Cuba, read the manuscript at a critical moment and offered her advice as she always does: directly, wisely, and caringly. Public historian Dominique Jean-Louis weighed in on the finer points of talking to children about difficult topics in history, a subject that has interested Dominique and Emma for many years, and Emma would like to thank her for her friendship, wisdom, and good cheer.

Adam would also like to extend his deep and enduring gratitude to Emma. Your thoughtfulness, care, and insights about children, literature, and Cuban-American culture have made this project richer and more beautiful than anything I could have imagined. It's also been a wonder to know you through your early writing career and PhD, to now, when I am honored and humbled to call you my collaborator—as well as my friend.

Additionally, Emma would like to thank her big Cuban family for their unwavering support and steady flow of good *chismes*, as well as her community of scholars and historians for their opinions, fact checks, and great conversations about identity and history.

A NOTE FROM EMMA

PEOPLE LIKE ME are always visiting Cuba in our imaginations. I was born in New York City at a moment when it was difficult to travel to Cuba, even to see close friends and family. But Cuba was at the heart of every story my family told, and so it became natural to imagine Cuba richly, to keep this place always close in my mind. My childhood was marked by the arrival of relatives from Cuba, people who I knew through stories but had never met: when they came to the United States, it was as surprising to me as it would have been for a character to walk out of a book. But the relationships my mom had with these relatives, and the new bonds I was forming, quickly proved that Cuba was more than a story. As policies changed, it became possible for my family and me to visit Cuba ourselves, and reconnect with friends and relatives there. Thanks to our family, friends, and friends-who-are-almost-family, I've had the chance to visit the streets, the sidewalks, the parks and the backyards of my parents' childhoods, and most importantly, to be with the people who matter to us. *Gracias, por recibirnos y apoyarnos siempre.*

I hope this book will give you a small taste of what it is like to grow up Cuban-American and what it is like to visit Cuba and have friends and family there. I hope you will learn a little bit about the United States' complex involvement with Cuba, and recognize that while ordinary individuals are often at the mercy of divisive policies, family bonds can transcend rifts, and that stories always do. Maybe because Cuba and my aunts, who existed for many years to me as fictional, turned out to be real, I trust stories and I trust family, and see in these the potential to bridge boundaries and distance. Thank you to all of the people who told me those stories, and all of the people who helped us write this one. Cuba is too big, diverse, and complex for any one person to tell her story. I encourage our readers to continue learning about Cuba through books, and I thank my friends, fellow writers, and scholarly community for their insights into this book.

—E.O.

Emma Otheguy is a children's author whose work focuses on Latin American history and Latino identity in the United States. She is the author of the award-winning bilingual picture book *Martí's Song for Freedom* (Lee & Low, 2017) about Cuban poet and national hero José Martí, as well as the middle-grade novel *Silver Meadows Summer* (Knopf, 2019), which Pura Belpré—winning author Ruth Behar called "a magnificent contribution to the diversity of the new American literature for young readers." Emma's forthcoming books include *A Sled for Gabo*, the first of two picture books with Atheneum, due out in fall 2020. Emma holds a PhD in history from New York University and has been the recipient of fellowships and grants from the Mellon Foundation, the American Historical Association, the Council of Library and Information Resources, and Humanities New York. Emma lives in New York City.

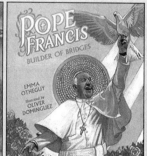

Adam Gidwitz taught big kids and not-so-big kids in Brooklyn for eight years. Now he spends most of his time chronicling the adventures of the Unicorn Rescue Society. He is also the author of the Newbery Honor–winning *The Inquisitor's Tale*, as well as the bestselling *A Tale Dark and Grimm* and its companions. He is also the creator of the podcast *Grimmest*.

Jesse Casey and **Chris Lenox Smith** are filmmakers. They founded Mixtape Club, an award-winning production company in New York City, where they make videos and animations for all sorts of people.

Adam and Jesse met when they were eleven years old. They have done many things together, like building a car powered only by a mousetrap and inventing two board games. Jesse and Chris met when they were eighteen years old. They have done many things together, too, like making music videos for rock bands and an animation for the largest digital billboard ever. But Adam and Jesse and Chris wanted to do something *together*. First, they made trailers for Adam's books. Then, they made a short film together. And now, they are sharing with the world the courage, curiosity, kindness, and courage of the members of the Unicorn Rescue Society!

Hatem Aly is an Egyptian-born illustrator whose work has been featured in multiple publications worldwide. He currently lives in beautiful New Brunswick, Canada, with his wife, son, and more pets than people. He has illustrated many books for young people, including *The Proudest Blue: A Story of Hijab and Family* by Ibtihaj Muhammad with S. K. Ali, the Newbery Honor winner *The Inquisitor's Tale* by Adam Gidwitz, the Unicorn Rescue Society series also by Adam Gidwitz with several amazing contributing authors, the Story Pirates book series with Geoff Rodkey and Jacqueline West, early readers series Meet Yasmin with Saadia Faruqi, and *How to Feed Your Parents* by Ryan Miller. He has more upcoming books and projects in the works. You can find him online @metahatem.